DRAMA QUEEN

DRAMA QUEEN

Chloë Rayban

BLOOMSBURY
CHILDREN'S
BOOKS

First published in Great Britain in 2004 by Bloomsbury Publishing Plc
36 Soho Square, London, W1D 3QY

A CIP catalogue record of this book is available from the British Library

ISBN 978 0 7475 6325 9

All papers used by Bloomsbury Publishing are natural, recyclable products
made from wood grown in well-managed forests. The manufacturing
processes conform to the environmental regulations of
the country of origin.

Typeset by Dorchester Typesetting Group Limited
Printed in Great Britain by Clays Ltd, St Ives plc

10 9 8 7

www.bloomsbury.com

chapter one

The morning we moved to Rosemount Mansions I picked every single daffodil in the garden and made them into a huge bunch to take with us.

'Couldn't you find something more useful to do?' asked Mum. She had her 'worried face' on. I could tell she was really upset. She was absent-mindedly picking things up and wrapping them in totally insufficient pieces of newspaper.

'Why don't you let the removal men pack those? They're being paid to do it.'

Mum put down the mug she was holding and looked defeated. 'Yes, I suppose you're right.'

'Come on. I'll make us a cup of tea.'

I went into the kitchen. The cooker had gone. There was just a gas tap sticking out of the wall where it had been. The electric kettle was still there. I filled it with water, plugged it in and looked around for the mugs, remembering, too late, that those had been what Mum had been wrapping. 'Where are the . . . ?' The box she'd been packing them in was already on its way down the drive to the van.

Mum sank into an armchair.

'Sorry, luv. But we're about to take that chair,' said a man standing over her.

So we made do with a family bottle of Coke, taking sips out of it in turn. We watched through the window as the potted plants, the last of our possessions, were on the move down the garden drive.

'Till Birnam Wood remove to Dunsinane . . . ' murmured Mum.

'What's that?'

'*Macbeth*.'

The foreman was leaning through the front door. He had a list in his hand. 'Can you sign this, luv?' Mum started scrabbling in her bag for her pen.

I wandered back up to my room. It was empty now except for a wicker cat basket with Bag asleep inside. There were pale rectangles on the wall where my posters had been. And the ghost of my bed traced in fluff on the carpet. I leaned on the windowsill and stared down at the garden. The daffodils had been the only patch of colour. Mum hadn't had the heart to do much gardening last summer. And Dad had never come to mend that bit of the fence that had come loose as he'd promised he would. Now the garden looked damp, overgrown and neglected, as if it had somehow absorbed all the misery of the past year. I wasn't sorry to leave.

I leaned down and hauled Bag (short for Bagpuss) out of the basket. He stretched and purred luxuriously in my arms. His fur smelt of dust and musk.

This was the room in which I'd woken up for all the Christmases and birthdays of my life. This was the room where I'd put on my first school uniform and thought it was the greatest day of my life – and to which I'd returned at the end of the day, older and wiser, having discovered what school was actually like.

It was here that Mum had come up and told me that Grandad had died and I couldn't think of anything to say. I'd had a dream that night in which I'd bumped into him at the fair and he'd held a finger to his lips and said, 'Don't tell Grandma, I want it to be a surprise.' I'd woken up thinking the dream was true.

This is where I'd hidden the basket with Bagpuss inside after I'd found him in the street. He'd been small enough to sit in my hand then. When Mum had found out she'd gone berserk but I'd pleaded and pleaded. She'd let me keep him in the end.

It was in this room that Dad had come and sat on the edge of my bed and said that he was moving out – for a while. Just as a trial . . .

'Jessica!'

'Coming.' I stuffed Bag back in the basket and did up the straps. Then after a last look around, I lumbered down the stairs with it.

Mum was standing by the front door with the keys in her hand. 'Are you absolutely sure there's nothing left upstairs?'

'Positive.'

'Maybe I should double-check?'

'Trust me! Let's go.'

We drove away. Mum didn't look back.

Rosemount Mansions. You could hardly find a greater contrast with the home we'd left. Everything back there had been neat and respectable and ordinary. A street where people washed their cars on Sundays and joined the local Neighbourhood Watch. The kind of street where, if you carried out a survey, it could represent the entire country, it was so crushingly average.

There was nothing ordinary about Rosemount Mansions. It was on the poor side of town. An area I'd passed through on the bus on the way to school and wondered about. There was a Caribbean supermarket that sold strange ethnic vegetables, an Indian deli and a Lebanese take-away with an endlessly rotating doner kebab. It was in the kind of street where people dumped supermarket trolleys or abandoned cars. There were always rubbish bags stacked on the pavement and there was a launderette on the corner where lost-looking people sat watching their washing going round and round, for what seemed like for ever.

The building itself, however, was amazingly gothic. It was tall, built in red brick, and it had somehow managed to collect every single style of architecture under one roof. At each corner there was a little fairy-tale tower with a witch's hat roof. Balconies sprouted in the oddest places – each with railings which had strange sinuous plants cast into them, looking as if some giant creeper had fallen under a spell and been changed into iron. The whole building was finished in ragged castle battlements from which bunches of London pride sprouted like windblown hair against the sky.

I'd been taken there with Mum by the estate agent. She'd sighed and moaned about how run down the place was. But I'd turned her attention to its finer points. Like the totally over-the-top lift at the end of the lobby which had ornamental brasswork decorated with scenes of knights on chargers and maidens with flowing hair. In the end she'd had to give in, because Rosemount was all we could afford.

We arrived that afternoon to find the removal van already parked outside. Most of our belongings were stacked on the cracked and broken front steps. The removal men had taken possession of the lift so we trudged up the umpteen flights of stairs that led to our flat. Bag's basket seemed to grow heavier with each floor. He was wailing as his nose met up with all the unaccustomed smells.

Our floor was the seventh – at the very top. The lift didn't even reach it. You had to climb a final set of winding stairs to get to it. The flat consisted of four low rooms tucked in under the battlements. Mum said it must have been the servants' quarters once – in the days when the people in the building were grand enough to have them.

The removal men were currently sweating and

moaning over that last flight of stairs. We forced our way through the queue of boxes into our front corridor.

'Oh my goodness, we're never going to get it all in,' said Mum.

'Where's this one to go, luv?' asked a man who'd got a box wedged between the washing machine and the doorframe.

'They should all be marked for each room,' said Mum. 'Where's my list?'

I left her to it while I took Bag on a tour of inspection. This didn't take long. Mum had the largest room which looked out on to a narrow light well at the back. Mine was all oblique angles and dramatically slanted ceilings with a view down on to the front entrance. Apart from the bedrooms, there was a kitchen, just big enough to hold a table, a balcony, just wide enough for Bag and his kitty-litter box, and a room we rather grandly decided to call the sitting room, which had enough space for the sofa, the TV and a small round table that used to be in Mum's bedroom.

This table was already standing in the bay window. Edging my way through piles of bedlinen and flattened boxes, I made for the kitchen. I found an empty jam jar, put the daffodils into it, and placed it on the table by the window.

Mum was leaning in through the doorway watching me with a strange expression on her face.

'What?'

'You are such an incurable romantic.'

'No I'm not.'

'Yes you are. How about that cup of tea now? I've relocated the mugs.'

'Is there enough milk for Bag?'

'Better not let him out till the men have gone. We'll have to butter his paws.'

'Butter his paws?'

'Yes. Makes a cat feel at home. Licking it off.'

'How weird.'

'I know. But it works for some reason.'

It was some six hours later that we actually got the place almost straight. With aching backs and cobwebby hair, we sat side by side on the sofa eating beans on toast. Bag was on the floor on a pile of newspapers washing butter off his paws. He kept pausing to lick his whiskers thoughtfully.

'I suppose it makes sense really. He only washes his paws when he's really contented, like after turkey at Christmas,' I said.

'Association of ideas,' said Mum. 'Butter breeds

contentment.' Bag had started to purr.

The sun had come out. A watery ray slanted through the dirty window and fell across the table. The daffodils seemed to light up the room. Mum leaned over to smell them. 'Heaven. We should've left them, really,' she said.

'Rubbish, the new people aren't moving in for a fortnight. They'd all be dead by then. Anyway, they'll have them next year. And the year after.'

'Yes,' said Mum and she looked very sad. I leaned down to stroke Bag, not wanting Mum to see I was upset too. 'I'll go and make some more tea,' she said. Her voice sounded funny.

I hated to hear her like that. Moving out had made it all so final. As long as we'd been in the old house, I could imagine that at any moment I would hear Dad's key turning in the lock and he'd come in and hang up his coat and everything would be back to normal.

Except it hadn't been normal, not for ages. I suppose I just remembered the good bits now. Like the daft jokes we shared and that holiday we'd had in that horrible stuffy mobile home when it had rained non-stop and we'd nearly worn out the Monopoly board. Dad and Mum hadn't been arguing much then. At least, not in front of me. It was difficult to place the time when it had started to go wrong. It was some-time after that holiday. They'd begun to have these rows, at least Dad had. He did all the shouting while Mum went all quiet. More recently the rows had got fewer and been replaced by long silences. Then they'd virtually stopped talking to each other. Whenever they said anything it was in a tired voice, as if they were making a tremendous effort. I know a lot of it was my fault. I'd shouted at both of them. And I'd sulked. I thought it would get through to them. I wanted to make them wake up and be normal again. But I'd only made it worse.

Then Dad had gone out a lot. He'd leave the house, slamming the door behind him and revving up the car in that exaggerated way I hated. Gradually he'd stopped coming back for meals – he just arrived late and went straight to bed. I think he used to eat in a pub, he always smelt of beer when he came to say goodnight. One day I discovered he was sleeping in the spare room. And then he started staying away at night. 'On business', he said.

Nine months ago he'd moved out altogether as a trial. The 'trial' went on for a month. And then another month. And then one day he took me out for that awful walk by the river and tried to explain that he was moving out for good. That he wasn't coming back ever. He was almost crying. I didn't know what to say.

'Tea up.' Mum's voice interrupted my train of thought.

I blew my nose and took the mug she offered.

Mum sat down on the sofa beside me. 'We'd better think how we're going to redecorate your room,' she said.

'You don't have to try and cheer me up.'

'You didn't *have* to bring the daffs,' she said.

I lay in bed that night listening to the traffic pass and watching the angled shadows of the headlights swing around my oddly sloping ceiling. A police siren wailed in the distance and a couple of cats started up an anguished chorus down below.

I wondered what the future would bring. I'd been flat out all day so hadn't even had time to check my mobile. I leaned over and raked it out of the bottom of my backpack. There was a text message from Clare.

welcome to your dream home
love wobble

I texted her back.

bag in basket, me in bed
sweet dreams
love j

chapter two

So our life at Rosemount Mansions began. I'd like to call it a turning point. And it was in a way.

We'd moved from the suburbs into the inner city. And while Mum moaned about the dirt and the noise and the lack of a garden, for me it was the start of something new and exciting. OK, so I'll let you into a secret. I've always had this ambition to be a writer. I don't tell many people because they think it's so un-cool. And I don't write much, because frankly my life back where we used to live was so-oo dull. What's there to write about when absolutely nothing happens?

But Rosemount was different. I loved the way the building seemed to have a life of its own. Whatever the time of day or night you could feel the buzz of other people's lives around you – the creak and slam of the lift door, a sudden burst of laughter, a baby crying or the purr of a taxi waiting outside. Every sound was a story about to happen.

From my viewpoint high up over the entrance, I could see whoever came or went. And long before I could match these aerial views of people to the names beside the doorbells, I had started making up imaginary lives for them.

'So what's the latest Rosemount news?' Clare would ask as I slid into the seat she'd saved for me in the bus. Clare lived in the nice quiet suburb we'd left. For her, my new inner city life was jam-packed with potential. Not much had happened so far. So I'd decided to make it sound more interesting.

'Another woman disappeared into number nine. Not seen to emerge. I'm watching to see if SK comes out with a large leaking suitcase.'

'SK?'

'Serial Killer.'

'Yukk. How about the clairvoyant in number one?'

(I didn't actually *know* she was a clairvoyant. I mean, she didn't have a crystal ball in her window or anything. But groups of people used to turn up in the afternoons and not emerge for hours. So I painted Clare a nice spooky picture of them inside, hand in hand around her table, calling up the dead.)

'Strange knocking sounds emerging from her flat. Blinds firmly closed.'

'Spotted any talent yet?'

'None so far.'

'How about the guy with the hairy wrists?'

'Mr Hyde? He's scary. His flatmate's not bad though. But we haven't established eye-contact.' (I'd seen each of these guys emerging from the same apartment on separate occasions. One with a black mac and hairy wrists, the other the same height and build but blond and blue-eyed. Never once seen together. Strange.)

Clare sighed. 'I thought the whole point of moving to a block of flats was all those encounters in the lift. Or on the fire escape.'

Clare's lack of love life was her constant obsession. Most of the other girls in our class had, or claimed to have, some male in tow. But whether it was the double brace, or the fact that she was so devoted to those shapeless tracksuit bottoms of hers, Clare never seemed to have any luck. I wasn't bothered myself – the boys who the girls in our class went out with were really immature. Personally, I preferred to remain single until I found complete *perfection*.

'So how on earth did *she* get *him*?' Clare nudged me and nodded in the direction of a curiously mismatched couple. A really fit guy was sitting beside a plain girl with lank hair.

'Maybe she's his sister.'

'They're holding hands.'

'Are they?' At that point the girl nuzzled up to the guy. 'I give up. I dunno. It happens,' I said.

'It's *so* unfair.'

'It's love. There's no logic to it.'

At that point we reached the stop for Westgate, our school. The bus disgorged its load of kids on to the pavement. Clare strode on ahead of me but I lagged behind, thinking about what I'd just said.

It's love – there's no logic to it. But there should be. Surely love is the most important thing in life? Who you ended up with couldn't simply be down to chance.

I considered the way the people up ahead of me were paired off. There was Marion, who'd been glued to Mark since nursery school – they were even planning to apply to the same colleges. And there was that boy in Year 9 with the big nose, whose name I never could remember, who'd teamed up with the girl with the dodgy legs. Then there were the drippy

Frinton twins who each had their totally uncool boyfriends. In fact, if you imagined a great cosmic game of Pelmanism, you could probably sort most of the people at school into matched pairs.

The school bell was already ringing as I reached the gates, so the last of us stragglers made a headlong dash for the doors, to avoid getting on the late list.

It was three hours later in a biology period while the teacher was droning on about 'natural selection' that the phrase came back to me again. *It's love – there's no logic to it.*

What was this curious process that attracted one person to another? Was it the survival of the 'fittest'? The bullfrog with the deepest croak gets the most frog wives. The strongest stag who can fight off all the other males gets the biggest harem. Were human beings just the same? All of us girls were after the 'fittest' male, after all. And all of the males were after the 'hottest' girl. Some people of course, sickeningly enough, attracted the opposite sex like filings to a magnet. But what about the rest of us? Did we just have to settle for what was left over? Maybe we were simply after the best we could get. We'd aim for the fittest but we'd then have to scale down our standards until we met someone who *we* thought were the best *they* could get.

It wasn't until double maths (not my best subject) that the answer to the whole thing came to me. I was studying this problem and the words literally leaped off the neatly squared page. 'Solve the inequality', it said.

Solve the inequality. That was it. Love is like a vast cosmic equation. The moment you meet someone of the opposite sex, your brain does this massive piece of mental algebra: i.e. his blue eyes and perfect teeth = my glossy hair and long legs.

be + pt = gh + ll   *Good Match!*

Then on a second glance you start to see negatives: i.e. his dodgy trainers and sticky-out ears.

be + pt – dt + soe < gh + ll   *Mismatch*

Errm. Maybe there should be some brackets in there somewhere. (Algebra was not my strongest subject.)

(be + pt) – (dt + soe) < (gh + ll)   *Better?*

But then you may have negatives yourself, i.e. my bitten nails and snagged tights.

$$(be + pt) - (dt + soe) = (gh + ll) - (bn + st) \quad Match!$$

Then, of course, the more you get to know someone, the more enters into the equation. Like ambition, for instance. He might want to be a brain surgeon, whereas I might just settle for being, say, a parking warden. So the equation would become unbalanced.

$$bs + (be + pt) - (dt + soe) > (gh + ll) - (bn + st) - pw \quad Mismatch$$

But it could be balanced back again if I was, say . . . about to become a rock star (just being a parking warden while I was building up my brilliant career). And then there were things like taste: whether you liked crap films and nerdy music. And whether you were knock-kneed or athletic. And loads of minor details to take into account, like whether you were incredibly miserly or disastrously spendthrift or rancidly untidy or pathologically orderly or could cook well or dance brilliantly or were tone deaf or . . .

'Jessica. Are you with us dear?' Ms Manson, the

maths teacher, was sitting at her desk beckoning to me. 'I asked you to come up so that we could go through last week's homework together.'

So I had to put my theory on hold till after school.

It was on the way home that the thought struck me. In fact, it actually stopped me in my tracks as I was going down the street towards Rosemount. If I was right about my theory, my *scientific* theory of love, then perhaps there were some things that could be substituted, on one side or the other, to balance the equation between Mum and Dad.

Like Dad minus pot-belly and dodgy taste in films, for instance, but plus a good book. Or by making Mum more glamorous: i.e. minus saggy cardie and frown lines and maybe plus make-up.

$$\text{Dad} - (pb + dtf) + gb = \text{Mum} - (sc + fl) + mu$$

Would *that* make them match up again?

I continued walking very slowly up our steps as I considered this carefully. Maybe if they could get them back into balance they could get back together again. They weren't divorced after all, only separated. There was still time.

I ran up the last few steps.

Bag was out on the balcony basking in the low after-noon sun and casting an assessing eye on the alley cats in the street below. I picked him up and he purred delightedly. Poor Bag, he'd spent all day alone. Maybe even he was searching for the perfect mate. Some low-life feral female who would ignore his saggy belly and cat-food-breath and appreciate him for his finer points.

B – (sb + cfb) = ?

I made myself tea, spooned out cat food into Bag's bowl and then wandered into Mum's room to check out her wardrobe. She must have some more flatter-ing clothes stashed away in there somewhere.

Rows of nondescript khaki and grey clothing met my eye. Several pairs of worn trainers, an odd sock and a jumper I hated had amazingly survived the move undisturbed, and were still lying, fluffy with lint, at the bottom of her wardrobe. On her dressing table there was a comb, a bottle of mass-market mois-turiser and a tube of lipsalve. The job of turning Mum into a love goddess was going to be an uphill task.

Bag, having finished his meal, had followed me into the room and was winding himself round my legs. 'What do you think, Bag?' He made no comment but climbed into the wardrobe, settled on the jumper and started to knead it with his paws, purring with ecstasy as if to say he liked Mum the way she was.

'You've no judgement whatsoever.'

I went back into my room to start my homework. The building was quiet at that time of day, waiting for darkness to fall before it came to life. I hauled files, set books and my pencil case out of my backpack and was arranging them on my table when I heard the resounding slam of the entrance door below. Someone had let themselves in.

I couldn't resist. I slipped out through our front door, tore down the stairs and peered down the stairwell. Six flights below me, swinging a knapsack of books in a way that suggested he belonged here, was a boy. I stood on tiptoe to get a better look. He was perhaps a little older than me. Not in uniform, so probably a sixth-former, but not from our school. Hmm, interesting. He was waiting for the lift. He got in and I heard its familiar wheeze and whirr as it started up. There was a hiss and then a jolt followed by the sound of the grille being opened and slammed shut again. I estimated he must have got out on around the third or fourth floor.

It hadn't really been possible to assess his potential from six floors up but I texted Clare straightaway.

stop press!
rosemount news!
talent spotted
love j

I started on my homework with a good feeling inside. I had an essay to do on *Romeo and Juliet*. Halfway through the first page, however, I started to run out of steam. I raided the biscuit barrel three times and ate two packets of crisps but I still felt positively hollow from hunger.

Where was Mum? She usually had some good tips on English essays. She was doing this Open University course. That had been one of the problems with her and Dad. She'd get all excited about some essay that she was doing and totally forget to cook dinner. It had driven Dad mad. And it drove her crazy that it drove him mad because she thought her

OU course was really important. More important than the dinner or the loo paper that she'd forgotten to buy or all the other things that went by the board.

Hang on a minute. It was Friday. I'd forgotten she had a rehearsal. Why had I ever had that totally irrational idea that 'amateur dramatics' would cheer her up? When I'd given her that: 'Why don't you get out and meet people' pep talk I hadn't realised that it would entail a stupidly late dinner twice a week. I stomped into the kitchen and opened the deep freeze compartment. A small pack of fish fingers and a bag of frozen peas met my gaze.

The over-microwaved fish fingers weren't too bad swamped in ketchup. Bag rejected the really tomatoey bits. I thought, grudgingly, of how all around me in the building, people were sitting down to meals together. *'Pass the roast potatoes, darling . . . Could you manage just one more slice of chicken breast? More gravy?'* (Gravy! Sigh . . . When did we last have gravy?) *'What's for pudding, Mum? Oh, homemade apple pie and cream! Yumm. How was your day? . . .'*

This reverie was interrupted by the sound of the lift arriving with a clunk just below. Mum let herself in carrying a jumbo size take-away pizza.

'Oh, you haven't eaten, have you?' she asked,

spotting my knife, fork and plate lying in the washing-up bowl.

'I was starving.'

'Sorry, traffic was a nightmare. Stop-start all the way. Friday night.'

'Doesn't matter. I'll have some pizza anyway. How was the rehearsal?'

'Total disaster. First run-through without scripts. Nobody'd learned their lines. George went ballistic. We've all got to be word-perfect by Tuesday. You wouldn't have time to test me, would you?'

'I've still got loads of homework to do.'

'Thirty pages to memorise. Goodness knows how I'm going to do it in time.'

'Honestly, it's only an amateur performance.'

'That's not the point.'

'I reckon he's a control freak. You're grown people, he treats you all like he does us at school.'

'He's the director. That's what he's there for.'

George, i.e. Mr Williams, was my English teacher. That's how Mum had come to join The Lansdowne Players. He'd put up a notice on the Arts Activities noticeboard announcing the auditions. When I caught sight of it I'd suddenly thought of Mum. She used to boast about all the acting she'd done at college. I gave the Players a big build-up to sell her the idea.

'If you're so keen, why don't you audition?' was her first reaction.

'I don't think I've got time. You know, coursework and everything. I've got so much homework this year.'

'You could manage it.'

I didn't dare admit the real reason. Frankly, I did-n't think I could endure the collective scorn of Year 11. You know, being in Mr Williams's amateur dramatics – just so-oo uncool.

'But *you* loved acting. You were really good at it.'

'Me? Rubbish. That was at least twenty years ago.'

'So?'

'You don't think I'm too old?'

'Old? No, it's a proper adult group.'

'Well, maybe I will.'

So Mum joined The Lansdowne Players. It was kind of weird hearing her refer to Mr Williams as 'George'.

Anyway, that night she went to bed early with her script. It was a play Mr Williams had written himself. Something historical and all in verse – nightmare! I could hear her muttering to herself through the door as I lay next door.

When I checked my mobile I found Clare had texted me back. Honestly, I reckon she must check her messages every five minutes.

re: rosemount talent!
more please?
age? height? hair/eye colour?
potential?
love wobble

I decided to let the suspense build up. Tomorrow would be soon enough; besides, I hadn't that much to tell. How much could one gauge from the top of a guy's head?

I lay in bed fantasising that he would turn out to be that *perfect* male I'd been looking for. The ultimate mix of Brad Pitt and Leonardo Di Caprio with Matt Damon eyes. We'd meet in the lift when I was looking really good in my new black jeans – must do something about my jacket . . . but maybe the weather would turn fine and I could just wear my new top . . . Anyway, we'd meet in the lift and he'd say something like:

'Hi. I'm Dan/Marc/Todd (Some really cool name, anyway). Haven't you just moved in?' And our eyes would meet . . .

(Mid-fantasy, I think I must've fallen asleep.)

chapter three

The next day, which was a Saturday, I got up really late. I'd ignored Mum's absurd suggestion that I might like to go to the supermarket with her. I'd given her 'Don't-lie-in-too-long' advice the grunt it deserved. 'And don't forget you're meeting your father for lunch,' was her parting shot.

When at last I surfaced, I found Clare had left three text messages. First:

urgent
ring me as soon as you're up!

Second:

more urgent
can we meet up later?

Third:

even more urgent!
have you died in your sleep?

I called her up around midday, while I was having a noisy breakfast in front of the *Saturday Show*.

'What's going on? Where are you? Is *he* with you?' she demanded.

I turned the TV down. 'Chill. All I know about him is his hair colour.'

'What is it?'

'Mouse. Now leave me alone. I'm watching a very important programme.'

But she continued to pester. I placated her with a promise to meet on the high street for a browse around the Mall before I met Dad.

Hauling myself off the sofa, I got ready. I stared at myself assessingly in the mirror as I did my make-up. Maybe this guy downstairs was going to be really fit. Living in the same building like this, I never knew when I might bump into him. I added a second layer of mascara just in case.

I'd pressed the button for the lift three times but nothing had happened. I could hear footsteps below and caught a glimpse of a hairy wrist sliding down the balustrade. It was Mr Hyde sweeping down the stairs in his long black mac. He was mumbling darkly to himself. Obviously the lift doors were jammed – again. Grumpily, I started my descent. There was an odd rattling and banging sound coming from somewhere. I tracked this down to the third floor where, sure enough, the lift doors were wedged open.

Inside, was the boy I'd seen from above the day before. And his bike. He'd balanced it vertically on its back wheel, the lift being too small to take the full length of it. He now had it stuck with the handlebars caught in the grille and himself trapped behind it.

Our eyes met.

Leonardo Di Caprio NOT. Brad Pitt NOT. Not even Matt Damon's eye*brows*. He had really dweeby square black glasses and his hair stuck up in a kind of tidal wave like Tin-Tin's. Still, he was young and he was local. So I swallowed my disappointment and said in a friendly manner, 'Wouldn't it have been a better idea to have carried that down the stairs?' realising, too late, that this was the last thing he wanted to hear.

He glowered at me and tugged at the handlebars. A hot red blush was spreading up from his neck.

'I just moved in upstairs,' I added, trying to make

up for my last comment.

'Oh?'

It was too late to redeem things now but I tried anyway. 'Can I help at all?'

'I can manage, thank you,' he said with dignity and started to twist the handlebars. There was a nasty grinding noise.

'Well. If you're sure . . .'

'I'm sure.'

I decided it would be kinder to leave him to it, so I continued on my way down. At the bottom, there was a huddle of people waiting for the lift.

A short man with a white military moustache, who looked just like Colonel Mustard, was repeatedly pressing the button. 'What's going on up there?' he demanded.

'Should we call the engineers?' asked a lady weighed down by supermarket carriers.

'A boy's got his bike stuck,' I said. 'You might need the fire brigade with cutting equipment.'

'Cedric!' said Colonel Mustard, and he started trudging up the stairs.

I was halfway across the common when I heard the 'tick, tick, tick' sound of a bike coming up behind me.

I didn't turn round. I heard the bike slow down. 'Cedric' came level with me.

'Hi.'

'So you got disentangled?'

'Uh huh.'

There was silence for a moment.

'Going to the high street?' he asked.

There was nowhere else I could be going actually, but I nodded anyway.

'Shopping?'

'Ah huh.'

This conversation wasn't exactly earth-shattering. In fact, as conversations go, it didn't even creep on to the bottom of the Richter scale. I slowed down, hoping he'd overtake. But he slowed even more.

I cast him a sideways glance. There are some people who should *never* wear Lycra cycle shorts. He was perched on his bike like an insect on a leaf. Dressed like this, complete with his cycle helmet, he looked exactly like a praying mantis. His bike was a racing model and he had those little leather straps to keep his toes in place on the pedals. It made idling the bike a tricky business. But he seemed determined to stick with me.

'So you've just moved in?'

'Mmm.'

'We're in number seven.'

'Oh.'

We'd reached the top of the high street by now and I noticed a group of Westgate girls standing on the opposite pavement. As luck would have it they'd spotted us. Oh no, it was Christine, star of Year 12, looking, as usual, at her best. Body to die for, endless legs, perfect hair. And *didn't* she know it. She was going out with a sixth-form boy called Matt from the private school on the common. Her male equivalent. Perfect pecs, Brad Pitt cheekbones, head of the school football team.

$$C + (btdf + el + ph) = M + (pp + BPcb + hsft)$$
Puke-making!

Christine looked over and spotted me with Cedric. Then she turned to one of the other girls and whispered something. All the girls stared in our direction. They obviously thought we were together. I had to think of some way to get rid of him. I slowed even more. He was ahead of me but going at a snail's pace, weaving his bike to and fro to keep balance.

'It's starting to rain,' he commented over his shoulder.

'Mmm.'

'You haven't got an umbrella.'

'No.'

'I could lend you my cycle mac.' He was already shaking out a crumpled piece of luminous yellow plastic.

'Thank you but no thank you.' Was I never going to get rid of him? I stopped and bent down to re-tie a perfectly tied shoelace. He continued weaving his way forward but, suddenly realising I was no longer with him, he turned abruptly to double back. Gravity was against this manoeuvre and it was too late to retract his toes. He subsided into a sad heap on the pavement. I walked on with as much dignity as I could muster.

The Westgate girls must've seen it all. It was so humiliating.

Once in the high street, I spotted Clare in the Body Shop. She was browsing through the natural hair conditioners trying to decide between aloe and avocado. Clare was so heavily into saving the planet, I reckon she'd drink her own bathwater if it would help cut pollution.

Dear Wobble, she never made an effort. Wobble was her nickname from when she was a toddler – the kind of nickname most people would hate. But the great thing about Clare was she didn't care. Typically, she was wearing her favourite shapeless grey tracksuit bottoms with the top knotted around her waist.

Her face lit up when she saw me and her dimples appeared like single quotes around her double brace. 'So have you had another sighting?' she asked breathlessly.

'Yes. As a matter of fact I walked across the common with him.'

Clare's eyes widened. 'Re-ally! Where is he?' She looked as if she was going to make a dive for the door.

'Cool it. He'll be miles off by now. He was on his bike.'

'So. What's he like?'

'Male and around our age,' I started, non-committally. It seemed such a pity to disillusion her.

'Fit?' she prompted.

I was just about to raise my eyebrows to heaven and give her a cruel but accurate lowdown, when I paused. A thought had struck me. I mean, if Clare was that desperate. Cedric, minus Lycra cycle shorts and dreadful haircut, might just equal Clare, minus saggy anorak and railway tracks.

$$Ce - (Lcs + dh) = Cl - (sa + rt) \quad \textit{Just maybe}$$

'Erm. He's called Cedric,' I started.

'Well, that's not his fault.'

I dredged my mind for the positives. 'He's quite tall. Nice brown eyes.'

'Go on.'

I was faltering now. 'Must be pretty fit. He's really into cycling. It's a racing bike.'

'Cool!' She'd moved on to testing the free perfume samplers. 'What do you think?' she asked, holding out a wrist to me.

'Well, if you want to smell like a fruit salad, it's your affair.'

That was the start of the Clare = Cedric experiment. It may seem a little callous to be using my own best friend as a guinea pig, but since it was all in the cause of science I reckoned I was justified. If it worked, she'd end up with a boyfriend, which is what she wanted. And if it didn't, nothing would've changed.

We continued on our way down the high street doing our usual Saturday morning window-shop. We always had this competition to see which of us could spot the most naff fashion object. Clare won with a crochet top which had plastic appliqué flowers on it. In fact, it was so naff it was almost cool.

I ended up by buying what my weekly allowance ran to, which was a special offer of really good hair conditioner from Superdrug. I left Clare arguing with the assistant as to whether or not their cosmetics had been tested on animals and headed for the park to meet Dad.

The church clock was striking two when I arrived, so I was fifteen minutes late – but Dad was always late anyway. I was already ravenous so I bought myself a bag of Monster Munch at the kiosk and sat on a park bench eating them by the pond. Mums and dads were bringing toddlers to feed the ducks. A boy and girl stood entwined at the water's edge. A pair of swans glided by in the distance. Swans mate for life, you know. I'd learned that in junior school Nature Study. In fact, today, everyone looked incredibly 'couply'.

I had plenty of time to observe the local scenery because Dad was late. Really late. I tried dialling up his mobile but, as usual, it went straight to his voicemail – he must have forgotten to charge it. Before he arrived I'd been to the refreshment kiosk three times and bought a muesli bar, a packet of crisps, and a packet of Werthers and demolished the lot. I'd even got to the point of wondering whether, for once in his life, he'd been on time and arrived as arranged at quarter to two and, not finding me there, had gone off. But then I caught sight of his familiar figure hurrying through the park gates.

'Hello,' he waved enthusiastically, scarf blowing in the wind, jacket undone, his hair blown back showing his bald bit. 'Bit late, sorry. Got held up,' he panted, hugging me to him. He felt round and warm and smelt of beer. I noticed that he hadn't ironed his shirt. The collar was all rucked up. I felt a wave of pity. He needed someone to look after him. I often dreamed that one day, maybe, when I'd finished school, I could share a flat with him. But then that would be so unfair on Mum. 'Cos she needed me too. More, maybe.

'Had to meet a chap about a bike,' he explained.

'A bike?'

'Motorbike. A Harley. Vintage. But only done 'bout fifty k.'

'But I thought you were getting a car.'

'Ah yes. But you see, I've always promised myself,' said Dad.

So I said, 'Cool.' And left it at that.

'Fancy something to eat?'

'Not wildly hungry really.'

'Sure?'

'How about you?'

'Not bothered if you're not. Hey, I bought you something.' He handed me a plastic bag. 'House-warming pressie.'

'Thanks.'

'I would've wrapped it, but . . . ' It was a battered supermarket bag, already used. Obviously something from a charity shop. I looked inside.

'Oh, it's lovely,' I said, hoping my voice didn't sound as falsely exaggerated to him as it did to me. It was a flowery pink quilted box with partitions inside. The sort of thing I hadn't liked since I was six, practically.

'For your dressing table, for hairgrips and stuff, you know.'

'Thanks, Dad.'

'So! What shall we do?'

I shrugged. 'Up to you. How about a film?' (We nearly always went to the cinema when we met up.)

'Want to see the bike? Check it out. Go to a film after?'

'Why not?'

We took the tube to somewhere miles out. But it gave us a chance to chat. I told him about Cedric's battle with the lift. And I was on the point of telling him about my scientific love theory. But something stopped me. If it was going to work on him, the less he knew the better.

The bike was in a run-down dealer's yard under some archways beneath a railway line. We dragged a man covered in grease out from under a car and Dad told him 'Mac' had sent him about the Harley. The man said it was out the back.

'Don't you think you're a bit, you know, old for a bike?' I suggested, as the thought sunk in that this was yet another nail in the coffin of our family life. I mean, you couldn't get three on a motorbike.

'No, no way.'

The bike was in a lock-up garage under wraps. The man took them off as if he was unveiling a work of art. Personally, I thought the bike had seen better days. It had a gash in the seat that had been sello-taped over. Dad brushed this off as a mere detail.

47

'We can redo the leatherwork,' said the man, wiping his hands on an oily rag.

Dad was leaning over the bike inspecting the underside. I could tell he was trying to sound knowledgeable as he reeled off questions.

'Could you start her up?' he asked. The bike made a very loud engine noise. 'Might have to take a look at the silencer,' he commented in an undertone to me. 'Can I take her for a spin?'

The man gave Dad a very straight look. He could obviously tell that Dad's lunch had been a liquid one. 'You got insurance?'

'Yeah, sure.'

'Got the papers on you?'

'Not on me, no.'

'Sorry, then. No can do. Come back another time.'

'What? But we've come all this way. Mac said—'

'How's about you come back a bit earlier in the day next time.'

Dad got his drift. He was flushing up. I could see the warning signs. At any moment there was likely to be a nasty row.

'Come on,' I said. 'We haven't got time, really. If we want to catch an early film we'd better get a move on.' I led him away still remonstrating about the inefficiency of some people. But personally I was relieved the guy wouldn't let him ride the bike.

'What did you think of it, eh?' started Dad when we were back on the tube.

'I'd hoped you might get a car, something I could learn on, when the time came,' I started.

'You can learn on your mother's car.'

Mum's car was on its last legs and had really dodgy gears that even she found difficult. 'Mum's car will be at the wreckers by then.'

'Well, maybe she'll have a new one by the time you start.'

'That bike smelt a bit when he started it up,' I commented.

'That's 'cos it's been off the road. A good run'd fix that. Damned annoying not being able to take it out.' He was flushing angrily again.

I changed the subject. 'What film shall we see?'

'Your treat. You choose.' He always said that.

I'd wanted to go to the latest romcom but I hesitated. There was no time like the present. If I wanted to change a few things about Dad, I might as well begin right away.

'There's a French film on at the Virgin. Everyone's raving about it.'

'Subtitles?' He sounded doubtful.

'I don't think there's much dialogue, actually.'

'Well, if it's what you'd like, Poppet.'

Predictably, Dad slept through most of the film. I kept on having to nudge him because he was snoring, and he'd sit up and pretend to start watching again.

As we walked back up the high street from the cinema, Dad took out a packet of cigarettes and lit one.

'I thought you'd given up.'

'I have, practically.'

'You're impossible.'

I'd promised Mum I'd be back by eight. Dad saw me to my bus stop and waited with me. The bus took ages. There was a gym opposite the bus stop. It had pictures of fit blokes pumping iron on the posters outside. I couldn't help being struck by the contrast with Dad.

'Where are you off to now?' I asked. I wondered what he did all that time in that grotty flat of his. It couldn't be much fun living alone.

'Oh, I don't know. Saturday night. Might go down the pub.'

(Might! I thought to myself.) 'Don't you ever do anything else?'

'Like what?'

'I wish you'd do something more active, that's all.'

'More active? What, for instance?'

I indicated the fit blokes on the poster. 'Look at those guys. You should get toned up a bit. You could join a gym.'

Dad shrugged. 'I'll think about it.'

My bus drew into sight at that moment. 'Well, don't . . . ' I was going to say, don't drink too much. But I knew that made him mad. And probably had the opposite effect.

'Don't what?' he asked with a frown.

'Look after yourself, Dad.'

He got what I meant. 'Sure. I will, Poppet. You look after yourself, too. Straight home now.'

Mum had washed her hair and was in her towelling robe drying it when I got home.

'Haven't done much about supper. Hope your dad gave you a good lunch,' she said between blasts of the hairdryer.

'Oh, yes. Yes, he did.' (Why did I always have to cover up for him?)

'Where did you go?'

'Umm. The Steak House,' I said, coming up with

the most plausible lie.

'Mmm lovely. What did you have?'

'Steak and chips . . . '

'And *garnish*?' (Garnish was one of our private jokes.)

'Two battered onion rings, a half tomato with fine herbs and three radish flowers.'

'Classic. Nice pudding?'

'Oh, apple pie and ice-cream.' Before she had a chance to interrogate further, I asked, 'Shall I blow-dry the back for you?'

'Would you? Then I'll make us a poached egg each.'

'Can I have two?'

'Of course. What film did you see?'

'*Etienne*. At the Virgin.'

'Really? What did your dad think of it?'

'He's not a total philistine, you know.'

'I never said he was.'

Over supper she asked me how I thought Dad was. I had a sudden picture of him, arriving late across the park, red in the face from drinking as usual. He was still smoking. And he had to do something about his weight.

'He's thinking of buying a motorbike,' I replied.

'Really?'

'Second-hand. Quite old, but it's a Harley-Davidson.'

'He's mad. Typical. So dangerous. I'll have to talk to him about it.' She stacked up our plates noisily in the bowl. I could tell she was really annoyed.

I watched her as she leaned over the sink. She'd stayed really slim. And with her hair just washed and shiny like it was now, you'd think from the back she was quite young. She must've looked like that when Dad first met her.

They'd met at a party. Mum was doing this course in social work – that's how she'd got the job she had now, in welfare. Or as Dad called it: 'Giving hand-outs to losers'. Dad worked in leisurewear wholesale. I don't know what he did exactly, but he was always boasting about these brilliant deals he'd made, which Mum called: 'Third World exploitation'. But in spite of their differences they'd fallen in love and got married and had a child – *me*. True love is meant to last for ever isn't it? So since theirs didn't, weren't they really in love after all?

That's when I thought of my theory again. If Dad and Mum had been a perfect match once, they must have changed. But not changed completely. They were still basically the same people. In order to get them back together again I didn't have to do that much. All I needed to do was substitute a few variables.

Currently Dad + beer belly + red face was not really a match for Mum + shiny hair + slim figure. In fact:

$$D + (bb + rf) < M + (sh + sf) \quad \textit{Mismatch!}$$

That's when I decided to start work on Dad.

chapter four

The next morning, Sunday, I was busy doing an English essay on one of our set texts – a play called *Pygmalion*. It was by someone called Bernard Shaw and was based on a classical myth about a king who fell in love with a statue which was transformed into a real person – his ideal woman. Or, as Clare put it more succinctly – it was basically *My Fair Lady* without the music.

Anyway, I reckoned there was something wrong with the play. Or to be more exact, about the ending. The play was about the relationship between this Professor – Higgins – and a girl who was a flower-seller, called Eliza. He was rich, famous, awesomely clever and incredibly posh and she was young and beautiful but had absolutely no class whatsoever. Or, to express it scientifically:

H + (r + f + ac + ip) > E + (y + b) – c   *Disaster!*

So, after a long and painful process of giving her a total makeover and transforming her into exactly what he wanted, i.e. young, beautiful, speaking posh and stylishly dressed:

H + (r + f + ac + ip) = E + (y + b + sp + sd)
Start buying confetti?

No way. He *dumped* her. *What a let down!* The play would have been so much better if they'd got together at the end.

Anyway. I was busy rewriting the end for Mr Shaw:

After the ball
Higgins: *Eliza, be a doll and fetch my slippers.*
Eliza: *Oh, Professor. Let me massage your feet for you.*
Higgins: *Ooh, that's lovely . . .*

I was just getting to the good bit when the doorbell rang. When I opened the door there was a woman standing outside who said, 'Hello. Is your mother in?'

I disentangled Mum from the vacuum and brought her to the door. There was a lot of nattering about us being new and who she was, which ended with, 'We wondered if you'd like to come down for a coffee? At number seven.'

(Number *seven*. This must be Cedric's mother!)

'Oh, how kind,' said Mum, brushing her hair out of her eyes. She ignored my warning glare and replied, 'We'd love to. When . . . now?'

'As soon as you like.'

'I'm doing my homework,' I mouthed to Mum from behind the door.

'Well, you can always finish it later, can't you?' Mum said.

Cedric's mum's flat smelt of floor polish and block air-fresheners. Cedric's bike was propped up in the hall on a kind of mat thing which was obviously custom-made for it. We were ushered into an icy drawing room. A proper tea set was laid with a plate of those assorted multicoloured biscuits that come in gift tins.

'My son, Cedric, will join us in a minute. He's just come in from a cycle ride.' There was the sound of a shower running.

There followed one of those excruciating conversations which are all questions and answers, in which we learned that:

1) Cedric's dad, Mr Jackson, like mine, was absent.
2) Cedric went to Cranshaw High – the private boys' school up on the common.
3) Cedric was destined to be a lawyer.
4) Cedric was in training for the school's cycle team.
5) *Cedric was obviously spoilt rotten by his mum.*

At which point the subject of our conversation entered the room. His hair was wet from the shower, which had somewhat tamed the tidal wave. It was now neatly parted and smarmed down flat on his head. He took one look at me and flushed scarlet.

'Oh, why didn't you put on your nice new jumper?' said his mum.

Cedric ignored this and went and sat on a chair as far away as possible from the table.

'Aren't you going to pass the biscuits round, Cedric?' asked Mrs Jackson.

Mum's eyes met mine and communicated a silent 'poor boy' to me.

'This is Jessica . . . ' said his mother.

'We already met,' said Cedric.

'Yes. Yesterday,' I said. 'In the lift . . . ' I immediately wished I hadn't mentioned the lift. 'When I was going shopping,' I ended lamely.

Mum and Mrs Jackson continued to talk about the building and its plumbing and the frequency of such things as rubbish collections. Riveting stuff. Cedric and I sat like two lemons in total silence.

'Cedric, why don't you show Jessica your record collection?' asked his mum. (*Record* collection? Vinyl? Pl-ease!)

''Cos just maybe she's not into 'jungle',' said Cedric in a tired voice. (He was so right.)

'No really, I can't stop,' I said. 'I ought to be getting back. I've still got stacks of homework to do.'

'Cedric does all his on Friday night so that he has the whole weekend free,' said Mrs Jackson.

(I was about to say that I might have something else to do on a Friday night, but thought better of it.)

'What a good idea,' agreed Mum, but gave me a raised eyebrow.

'Well, thank you for the coffee . . . ' I said, backing towards the door.

'Won't you have another biscuit?' asked his mother in a last-ditch attempt to keep me there.

'No, really, thank you. I couldn't.'

'Show Jessica out, Cedric,' ordered his mum. Cedric reluctantly hauled himself off his chair and went towards the door. We reached the doorway at the same time and had a really embarrassing 'you first' session. 'Ladies first, Cedric,' called out his mum.

In the hall, he unlatched the front door and held it open for me. 'Sorry about my mum,' he said, looking really embarrassed. 'She means well.'

'Mine drives me mad too at times.'

'That's what mums were made for, I guess.'

'Well, see you round,' I said.

'Inevitably.'

'Mmm.'

Mum arrived back about ten minutes later.

'I thought I'd never get away,' she said. 'That poor boy.'

'Smother love,' I agreed.

'If I ever get like that, please tell me.'

'You won't. You couldn't.'

'Really?'

'I'd have left home long ago.'

* * *

60

I returned to my *Pygmalion* essay. I was rather pleased with it, actually. I finished the last act with Prof. and Mrs Higgins (i.e. Eliza) having breakfast one sunny morning in their thatched cottage in Surrey with Eliza expecting the first of their four perfect children. I put down the last word, 'Curtain', with a flourish. George Bernard Shaw eat your heart out. I had righted an injustice.

Next morning, Monday, I stowed the essay away in my backpack with care. Mr Williams was going to be impressed. I expected that he'd give me at least an A+ for it. I set out for school with a good feeling. This mark should go towards my GCSE coursework.

Downstairs, I stopped in the lobby to check the post. There were a load of bills addressed to Mum. And another envelope. A purple one, the kind that came with greetings cards. It was addressed in neat black handwriting to Miss J. Seymour, Flat 12, Rosemount Mansions, SW12 4QU.

That was odd. It was our address, all right. But the people who'd lived here before us had been called Hill. And they'd had all their post redirected. I checked down the names beside the other mailboxes. There was no one called Seymour in our block.

Obviously someone had got the wrong address. In which case the best thing to do was to put it back in the postbox and hope the postman would recognise the name and redeliver it. I took out my pen and scrawled on the envelope, 'Not known at No. 12.' That should do it. I glanced at my watch. One minute to get to the bus stop. I thrust the envelope into my bag and ran.

The bus drove up with Clare waving enthusiastically from the upper deck. I climbed up to join her. She was bursting for news.

'Did you see him over the weekend?'

'Him?'

'Cedric!'

'Oh, *him*. Yes.'

'Well?'

'I was invited over to his place.'

'Really.'

It was going to be tricky to cover up the total uncoolness of this visit. 'He's got a fantastic record collection.'

'*Records?* Like what?'

'Well, all sorts, you know.'

'More specifically?' demanded Clare.

'Jungle, mainly.'

'What's that?'

'Some pretty cool stuff that was round in the late 90s,' I said.

'So when am I going to get to meet him?'

'What about inviting him to Marie's party?' I suggested.

'What, just like that? Out of the blue? Won't he think that's a bit odd?'

'Well, maybe we should get to know him a bit better first.'

Clare frowned considering the problem. 'Perhaps we could bump into him on the way back from school,' she suggested.

'He goes to Cranshaw. It's totally in the wrong direction.'

'Where does he hang out?'

'Errm. I think I saw him once in Costa's.' (Costa's is a really cool coffee bar that recently opened in the high street. I mean, I have seen Cranshaw guys in there. He could well have been with them.)

'We could sit in there for ever, and their coffee costs a bomb.'

'Umm.'

'Tell you what. I'll come over to your place and check him out.'

'But we can't just ring on his doorbell.'

'We could bump into him *accidentally*.'

'We'd have to hang out on the stairs all day.'

'We could wait in your flat and then lure him up.'

'But how . . . ?'

'I've got it. Chocolate brownies!' she announced. 'They never fail.'

'What?'

'When a male gets the scent of chocolate in his nostrils, all hot and rich and gooey – he's dead meat.'

'How do you mean?'

'Listen, we get back from school before him, OK? We get them cooking. A great whoosh of fresh hot brownie smell down the lift shaft. Then one of us bumps into him by accident – he'll be upstairs in no time.'

'If you think so.'

'I know so.'

Friday afternoons we always got off early. Armed with a pack of brownie mix, Clare's best new jeans and her boots with heels, we were ready for action.

'OK,' I said, as soon as we were in my flat. 'You get changed first while I start the brownies.'

I found a mixing bowl and Mum's electric whisk

and studied the oven. It was a gas one with all sorts of safety devices. Mum had been moaning about it for days, saying that she just couldn't work out how to use it. It looked simple enough to me.

Clare was going the whole hog. I could hear water running and there was a sickly smell of cocoa butter bathfoam wafting out of the bathroom. I glanced at the clock. Twenty minutes till lift-off!

I couldn't find anything to measure the water with, so I slopped in what looked like five fluid ounces and switched on Mum's whisk. The mixer blades were hardly making any impression on the mix so I added a bit more water for luck. Suddenly it was all going horribly runny, so I lifted out the mixer which spun a great arc of chocolate rain all over me and the kitchen. Ooops! Still, no time to lose. I could always clean up later. I raked in the cupboard for a baking tray.

'How's it going?' called out Clare.

'Fine! You nearly ready?'

'Aren't *you* going to get changed?'

'Must get this in first.'

Slam, bang, crash. I had to take out every single saucepan until I found a measly little sponge tin at the bottom of the cupboard. I poured in the brownie mix which overflowed in a great brown slick on the worktop. Oh dear. Still. Yumm, tasted nice anyway. Shoving the tin in the oven, I turned my attention to the frosting. Thankfully there was a sachet of ready-made which I squeezed out into a bowl. Right, that was done. I dived into my room to change.

I couldn't find my jeans anywhere. Mum must've hung them up. Or taken them to wash. My room soon looked in a similar state to the kitchen.

'Looks as if there's been a massacre in here.' Clare's voice came from the kitchen. 'And they don't smell as if they're cooking.'

'Better turn them up then!' I yelled.

'Are you keeping an eye on the front?'

'Yep. No sighting yet,' I called back, hauling on a pair of tracksuit bottoms. Very unsexy! But it was Clare who mattered.

I came back into the kitchen. She was right, not the least whiff of brownie. I peeped in through the oven door. Sure enough, the oven had done one of its 'safety first' acts and turned itself off.

'Keep an eye on the front and I'll deal with this,' I instructed Clare.

'Right!' I told the oven. 'You asked for this.' I turned it on full blast and, as an extra measure, I also turned on a knob that said 'Grill'.

'There's a boy coming now, but I don't know if it's him,' called out Clare.

I dashed to my window. The boy she'd seen was delivering flyers. He paused to dump a load by our mailboxes and then walked off.

'No. Anyway, Cedric's taller.'

'How will we know whether or not to invite him?' Clare suddenly asked.

'We'll have to have some sort of sign.'

'Like what?'

I thought for a moment. 'I've got it. If you like him enough to invite him, you eat a brownie. If you don't, you don't.'

'So if neither of us eats a brownie, we don't invite him?' said Clare.

'Right.'

'What if one of us does and the other doesn't?'

'Hmm . . . problem.'

'I know! The one who *really* wants him to come, eats two.'

We agreed on that. The delicious warm rich smell of brownies was just starting to waft from the kitchen. But there was still no sign of Cedric.

'Maybe we've missed him,' said Clare.

'I don't see how we could have.'

'Maybe he got off early or he's gone somewhere after school.'

'That would be just our luck. Hang on, there's a bus coming from the Cranshaw direction.'

Sure enough, a minute or so later, Cedric came into sight.

'Right! That's him. Action stations!' I said. 'Keep fanning out the brownie smell and I'll go down for him in the lift.'

This announcement coincided with an agonising electronic bleeping. 'What's that?' gasped Clare.

'Smoke alarm! Oh my God!' We leaped for the hallway. Smoke was billowing out of our kitchen door. 'Open the front door. No, don't. Oh God, what shall we do?'

'Turn off the oven!'

'I can't. It's too smoky!'

'We better get out of here.'

We were about to make a dash for it, when I suddenly realised 'Bag!' I raced into my room and scooped him up from my bed. We collided with Cedric as we left the flat. He must've run up the stairs to see what the commotion was about.

'What's going on? What's that burning smell?' He

forced his way past us into the kitchen and flung open the window. The smoke quickly thinned. Then he climbed up on a chair and deftly took the case off the smoke alarm. There was a welcome silence.

'They're always doing that,' he said. 'All these flats have the same smoke alarms. They overreact . . . ' He opened the oven door, fanning the smoke towards the window.

'Jeesus. What happened in here?' he said, looking around the kitchen.

'We were cooking,' I said lamely. 'Oh, and by the way. Cedric, this is Clare.'

'Hi!' she said. Her face lit up, showing off her dimples to full advantage. 'We've just made a batch of brownies. Would you like some?'

There you go. She really liked him. Well, I suppose in the situation, he was being quite masterful.

I took the oven gloves and hauled the baking tray out of the oven. They looked more like 'blackies' than 'brownies'. I sent Clare and Cedric to put some music on while I did a quick camouflage job with the bowl of chocolate frosting. Arranged artistically on a plate they didn't look too bad.

'We need tea,' I called out.

'I'll make it,' said Clare. She looked really pretty

when she smiled like that. Those dimples were obviously having a positive effect on Cedric.

'I'll help you,' said Cedric.

I left them to it and took the plate of brownies into the sitting room. Things got really promising over the tea-making. Cedric and Clare discovered the bowl of frosting. I mean, it kind of deteriorated into a food fight. But then, you'd never splatter chocolate frosting over someone you didn't fancy, would you?

They came back armed with three mugs of tea. Cedric picked up a brownie and took a big bite. There was an odd crunching noise. I bit into mine. It tasted like coal but I munched on regardless. Clare was licking the frosting off hers, which was really confusing. Was that a 'yes' or a 'no'? I eyed her and chewed my brownie with determination. She'd put hers down. I glared at her meaningfully and took another. Somehow I choked it down. I kicked her under the table. Our eyes met. She nodded.

'There's a party at this friend of ours, Marie's place . . . ' I started.

The words were hardly out of my mouth before Cedric had taken our mobile numbers, given us his, offered to bring a bottle and checked out what he should wear. Clare looked over the moon. How simple it was to plant the seeds of love.

Now all I had to do was extricate myself from the equation. We were currently:

Clare + Cedric + Jessica   *Triangle*

When we should be:

Clare + Cedric − Jessica

i.e.:

Clare = Cedric   *Nice Match!*

I watched them together: Cedric was telling Clare about his bike and she was drinking in every word. (Sweet. They had forgotten I even existed.) Slipping out of the room, I pretended to make a start on cleaning up the kitchen. I could hear little snatches of their conversation through the open doorway.

' . . . I changed the main frame right away.'

'Uh-huh?'

'I can get it up to around 20 k on the flat.'

'Re-ally?'

'More with the wind behind.'

'Don't you need special tyres?'

'Umm, and the shock absorbers, they're nothing like a normal bike . . . '

'I love cycling . . . ' I heard Clare say. (As far as I could remember, her pink and silver Raleigh hadn't been out of the shed since we left junior school.)

Cedric left us with the suggestion that we all meet up for a cycle ride sometime. I agreed enthusiastically, not mentioning the fact that I didn't have a bike. Which would mean, of course, the two of them would have to go without me.

I lay in bed that night feeling a nice cosy glow of satisfaction. It was so easy getting people together. Clare and Cedric were clearly made for each other. Everything confirmed my theory – it was just a matter of balancing their equation. I imagined sorting out people's lives on a global scale. Starting with Mum and Dad of course, and then working outwards. If everyone could be matched to someone, the world would be a much happier place.

The news is always full of human misery, isn't it? But if everyone was happily paired off with their perfect partner they wouldn't want to go round fighting wars and bombing people, would they? I imagined the headlines in my new improved world:

Twenty million, nine hundred thousand and
ninety-nine Britons arrive home safely

Seventy thousand Boeing 747s land without incident

No one murdered in the East End

Eleven thousand healthy babies delivered

Forty-seven countries at peace

chapter five

It was about a week later, while I was raking through my schoolbag in the vain search for a stray ink cartridge, that I came across the purple envelope again. Oops! I had totally forgotten to drop it in the post.

I turned it over. There was my message: 'Not known at No. 12.' Well there was no way the post could return it as there was no sender's address on the back. And ten days later it was hardly going to arrive 'on the day', was it? So there really wasn't much point in re-posting it.

I was about to throw it in my waste bin when I thought better of it. Sometimes greetings cards from people, like grandparents for instance, have cheques in them. In which case it would be wrong to just chuck it out. And maybe there might even be an address inside. So I tore open the envelope.

'*To someone special . . .*' it said on the front of

the card. I opened it and read the following:

Dearest darling Jane

In life as in art
You've stolen my heart
The moment you're free
Will you marry me?

Henry

My heart did a double somersault. *Marry me*! O-m-G, what had I done? Or rather, what *hadn't* I done, forgetting to re-post it like that? Poor Henry, whoever he was. Nightmare! What could I do now? I picked up the envelope again. It was definitely addressed to Flat 12, Rosemount Mansions. Our flat.

I went hot and cold. I felt really guilty. This Henry person might be suicidal on not hearing back from Jane. Imagine them meeting up and her not saying anything, as if she were purposely ignoring the letter. And him feeling totally rejected. (Like I did that time I thought I'd established eye-contact with that really cool guy in Virgin Megastore and then found he was eyeing up the girl behind me.)

And what about this Jane person? She must have had an inkling that Henry was about to 'pop the question'. So she's been waiting helplessly, hopelessly. Maybe she was about to do something drastic. It was just like that awful bit at the end of *Romeo and Juliet*, when you know that if only that letter had got to Romeo in time, it wouldn't have ended that way. And it was so frustrating.

I stared at the envelope. There was no easy way out of this one. In the circumstances, I could hardly drop the letter back in the postbox and hope for the best.

Who was Jane? I tried to picture her. She was blonde, I decided. She had straight blonde hair and pale skin – blue eyes of course. A slim willowy sort of perfect cross between Gwyneth Paltrow and Meg Ryan. But where was she? And how could I find her?

There must be a way. If this were a criminal investigation, I'd be giving the evidence forensic tests. I sniffed the envelope. It smelt of the banana that had been beside it in my schoolbag. I turned the card over and looked at the back. 'Hallmark' it said, unhelpfully. It was a pretty popular brand of card. Hardly worth questioning all the stationers in the district, like they do about guns, checking who they might have sold it to.

But maybe Jane *was* somewhere in the building. I needed to double check the mailboxes. I went down in the lift to take another look. This confirmed that there was no box marked 'Seymour'. There wasn't even anyone with the initial 'J'.

Back in my room I stood and stared out of the window searching for inspiration. The telephone directory was the most obvious first step. Maybe I could find a J. Seymour with a similar address to ours.

I located our directory lurking among a pile of magazines and turned to the 'S' section. Selkirk, Selwyn, *Seymour*. There were an awful lot of them, Seymour is a pretty common name. There were quite a number of J. Seymours too but none of them had an address that was anything like ours.

The moment you're free, the card said. Maybe she was married, or she might be living with someone else. In which case she could still be somewhere in our building and it was merely a case of someone having got the wrong flat number. Clearly, I would have to start my research from square one.

I decided to drop in on Cedric. He said he'd lived at Rosemount all his life, so he should know of

'J. Seymour' if anyone did. I made my way downstairs and rang on his doorbell. After a moment's pause I heard the sound of footsteps from inside. The spyglass went dark and I could tell someone was peering through.

'Hi!' I tried.

But the door didn't open right away. Odd. I waited another minute or so and then rang the bell again, harder this time. There was a sort of scuffle the other side, then Cedric swung the door open with a flourish.

'Hi!' he said. He'd obviously just gelled his hair. The tidal wave was sticking up vertically as if he'd had an electric shock. The strength of his aftershave nearly knocked me flat.

'Come on in,' he said.

I stepped inside.

'What's up?' asked Cedric.

'I just wondered. I mean, you've lived here for ever. Have you ever heard of anyone called Jane or Seymour living in the building?'

'Seymour . . . don't think so. Like a cup of coffee? Tea? Why do you ask?'

'It's just that a letter arrived for her. Misdirected to our address.'

He shook his head. 'Coke. Lemonade?'

I followed him into the kitchen. 'No, really, thanks.'

He opened the fridge door. 'Orange juice?'

'Well, maybe . . . '

Kicking the fridge door closed with his heel cowboy-fashion, he flipped open the orange juice with his thumb, grinning at me in an over-confident manner. 'Jane *who* did you say . . . ?'

'Seymour. Maybe it was someone who stayed with the Hills when they lived in our flat?'

'Can't ever remember anyone staying. They were really quiet. Kept themselves to themselves.'

'In another flat then?'

'Not that I can remember. There's a girl in number six. She's new. Don't know her name.'

'What's she like?'

'Dunno. She's got a baby.'

'Is she married?' I asked.

'Haven't seen a bloke around.'

(My mind was racing. Maybe Jane and Henry had got separated. Yes . . . They'd broken up and Henry had left the country, or been swept away at sea, or lost his memory. Any of those standard things they use to get rid of fathers in soap operas. And Jane had been left struggling to survive alone . . .)

Cedric had located two glasses and was leaning up against the fridge. He gave me a sideways look: 'What are you doing later?' he asked.

I was suddenly struck by the awful thought that he might think my story of the lost letter was an excuse to see him. Oh no, surely not. I mean Cedric was fine for a *friend*. I don't want to be arrogant, but standing there in his hideous shiny shellsuit bottoms, he was no match for me, even on my very worst bad hair day.

Cedric + hssb < Jessica + vwbhd   *Pl-ease!*

'Clare said she might drop by,' I improvised. (I could always call her.)

'When?' he asked.

''Bout six, I think.'

He glanced at his watch. Not a good move when holding a carton of orange juice. When we'd finished sponging juice off ourselves, he suddenly blurted out, 'I was thinking of going to see *Terminal Crime*. It's on at the MGM.'

'Really?' (*Terminal Crime* was a really gory suspense movie. I'd been trying to avoid it actually.)

'Maybe you'd like to come along?'

(*You?* This was obviously meant to be '*You*' plural,

80

i.e. me *and* Clare. Too shy to ask Clare on her own, I guess.) So, in spite of the fact that *Terminal Crime* was the last thing I wanted to see, I said, 'Why not. What time?'

'8.40.'

'Great. Meet you outside.' He let me out of the flat and I made my way upstairs, still wondering uneasily about that sideways look. No, it was Clare he was after, I told myself firmly – I'd been imagining things.

I rang Clare right away. 'Can you make the 8.40 at the MGM?'

'To see what?'

'*Terminal Crime.*'

'But you said you didn't want to see it.'

'I know. But guess who's going to be there?'

'*Cedric?*'

'Uh huh?'

'How did you manage that?'

'He suggested it. I reckon it's so that he can see you.'

'So why didn't he ask me himself?'

'I think he would have done if I hadn't dropped by.'

* * *

Still having a couple of hours to kill, I decided to use my time constructively and check out the girl in number six. It all fitted. I was starting to build up the story in my mind. Jane and Henry must have split up. Maybe he didn't even know about the baby. But someone must've told him. Now, realising that he couldn't live without Jane – and the baby of course – Henry was trying to get back together with her. And I was about to reunite them.

I paused outside the door, feeling the full significance of the occasion . . . but wondering how best to introduce the subject. I had just raised my hand to ring on the bell when the door was flung open.

This was no perfect Gwyneth Paltrow/Meg Ryan clone. The girl facing me had a wild expression and her hair was all over the place. Her clothes looked as if she'd slept in them.

'Yes?' she snapped, glaring at me.

She'd put me totally off my stroke. 'I . . . umm. I mean, I'm trying to track someone down . . . '

There was an ear-piercing screech from inside the flat. The girl disappeared from sight and re-emerged carrying a baby. I stared at the baby. Henry was in for a shock here. This baby was of the less attractive kind

– the blotchy, red and runny-nosed variety. If I were Henry, I'd stay well away until it reached a reasonable age.

A sudden noise of water gushing from an overboiling saucepan came from inside the flat. 'Oh my God. Hold him, can you?' She thrust the baby into my arms. It took one look at me and emitted another painful scream – obviously didn't take kindly to being planted on strangers. More screams followed, telling me in no uncertain terms that the sooner I handed it back the better. I tracked the girl down to a kitchen that looked as if it had been recently vandalised.

'Sorry . . . ' she said, leaning exhaustedly on the kitchen table. 'You were saying?'

The baby had taken up a steady howling. 'I'm from upstairs. Number twelve. I'm trying to track this person down,' I shouted above the noise. 'A letter came to our flat, wrongly adressed.'

'What?'

'You wouldn't be called "Jane", by any chance?'

'No, Roz. My name's Roz,' she shouted back.

I thrust the baby back into her arms. 'Thanks, that's all I wanted to know. I'll let myself out.'

I shut the door thankfully against the volume of screams. Poor thing, I thought. Trying to manage all on her own. What she needed was a man around. Someone sensitive and caring, like Jekyll perhaps – or even Hyde . . . They lived in the same building. All they needed was someone to bring them together . . .

I got ready for the cinema, plotting ways to help them meet up.

As luck would have it, when Clare and I joined the queue, who should be four people ahead of us but *Christine*. I really didn't want to be seen with Cedric. I just prayed she'd get in ahead of us and that we'd be able to smuggle him in under cover of darkness.

Christine was alone and kept looking round behind her. She tossed her perfect hair and gave us just a *half* smile of recognition. She was obviously waiting for someone. Matt probably. Sure enough, after a few minutes he came swinging down the street. Every girl in the queue visibly perked up. He joined Christine with a big public display of affection. All of us ordinary mortals sank back into oblivion.

The film was really popular. The attendant kept on coming out and counting the queue. People were being admitted in batches. We were just about to get inside when Cedric showed up. Or to be more precise, his bus drew up. And Cedric, while trying to wave, nearly got carried on to the next stop. He jumped off, causing a hooting commotion as he narrowly missed getting run over by the car behind. Great entertainment value for the queue. He should have taken a hat around.

'Hi!' he said to Clare. (Feigning surprise at seeing her with me.) People behind us were starting to get restive at yet another person joining the queue ahead of them. 'Maybe I should go to the end,' said Cedric.

'No way,' said Clare, taking him possessively by the arm. 'We were saving a place for you. Weren't we?'

I nodded.

A guy behind us sneered at Cedric, 'I've been standing here for half an hour, mate. If I don't get in, you'll be sorry.'

'Yeah, right, I'm going to the back right now . . .' said Cedric, tugging himself free.

'No, you're not,' said Clare, grabbing him again. She turned to the guy behind. 'I don't suppose you've ever kept a place for anyone,' she said. ''Cos who would want to sit with you?'

He then started on a stream of insults.

'Don't take any notice,' said Clare to Cedric.

At that point we got to the head of the queue and

were allowed through to the ticket desk. We were the last to be let in. The guy behind us totally lost it. 'I'll see you outside, after the film,' he bellowed after us. We ignored him with dignity.

Once inside, I positioned myself strategically so that Clare was in the middle, and Cedric on the other side of her. The film was pretty scary. I noticed Clare was actually clinging to Cedric. Or was it Cedric clinging to Clare? Anyway, it was first-class bonding material.

We emerged from the cinema feeling shaken and jumpy. Clare and Cedric got deep into a discussion over the goriest details. Since I'd had my eyes shut for at least fifty per cent of the action, I didn't have much to contribute.

We were just making our way down the high street when the guy who'd been behind us in the queue appeared from out of the shadows. 'Enjoy the film?' he sneered at Cedric.

Cedric cleared his throat. 'Bit predictable, actually,' he said. His voice sounded kind of squeaky.

'Bit pre-dic-table,' echoed the guy in a nasty sarky tone. He started tailing us. He was a bit older than us, a lot shorter than Cedric, but built like a tank. We stepped up speed considerably. But he still caught up with us. He grabbed hold of Cedric's jacket, swinging him round. 'Wanna come'n tell me 'bout it?' he snarled.

Clare got between them. 'Get your hands off him,' she demanded. 'You could be had for assault for that.' I stared at Clare. I'd never seen her being so assertive before. The guy had already let go his hold and was backing away as she continued. 'We're witnesses. I know who you are. You go to my brother's school, don't you?'

'What are you? His bodyguard?' said the guy with a half-hearted laugh, but he had already turned and was making his way back up the street.

'Jeez, Clare, well done,' I said.

'Wow, not bad for a girl,' said Cedric, pulling his jacket back on.

'Any time,' said Clare.

'Does he really go to your brother's school?' asked Cedric.

'I haven't got a brother,' said Clare. 'But he didn't know that.'

I usually stayed over at Clare's when she and I went out on a Saturday night, but I wanted her and Cedric to have some time alone together, so I suggested that

I took a cab while Cedric saw Clare home. But Cedric pointed out that it would be easier if Clare took a cab, since *we* were both going back to Rosemount. And then Clare stupidly said that if Cedric was with me, I wouldn't need a cab so wouldn't have to fork out for the fare. But I nobly said I didn't mind. Which ended in one of those stupid circular conversations where no one could make their mind up. Eventually we decided on a round trip by bus, taking in a coffee at Clare's.

Back at Clare's I went to her room to sort out the music, leaving the two of them alone to make coffee. I could hear them bantering away happily in the kitchen. I reckoned the whole episode with the guy in the queue had thrown them together.

I had confirmation of this on the way back to Rosemount.

'So what do you think of Clare?' I asked Cedric.

'Some girl,' he said, raising his eyebrows.

'She's really into jungle,' I prompted.

'Really? Who?'

'All kinds. She'd love to hear some of your stuff.'

'Would she?'

'Yeah. You ought to ask her round.'

'Maybe I'll do that.'

* * *

It was well past midnight when I got home. I noticed Mum's light was still on. I peeped round her door. She must have fallen asleep learning her lines. She still had her glasses on and the script for the play was on the duvet. I lifted it gently from under her hands so as not to wake her. I was in half a mind to read it through to see just how bad it was. But it was late and I was pretty tired so I thought better of it.

Mum half woke. 'Why didn't you stay at Clare's?'

'Cedric brought me back.'

'That was nice of him. Goodnight,' she murmured sleepily.

chapter six

The next morning I woke to hear the phone ringing and Mum answering it. I strained my ears. It was obviously Dad on the phone. He was sounding off at Mum about something. She came into my bedroom to wake me up with her 'tired look' on.

'What was that all about?'

'Dad went spare about me being out at rehearsals on Friday night. Seems he thinks you nearly burnt the building down.'

'Oh, for goodness sake. I only mentioned I just a-tiny-weeny-bit overcooked a batch of brownies.'

'He said, you said that the smoke alarm went off.'

'It did. So?'

'Well, it could have been serious.'

OK, I'd had this before. Each of them showing the other how to be the ideal parent. Which basically meant treating me like a child.

'Well, it wasn't, was it?'

'Maybe I shouldn't be out so much.'

'Don't be daft. It's only two nights a week.'

'Oh, I don't know.'

'Look, if something did go wrong, it's safe as anything in a building like this. There are always loads of people around.'

'Yes, I suppose you're right.'

'It's just Dad being paranoid.'

'It's Dad being *something*,' she said.

I had to be more careful what I told Dad. Edited highlights of my life would do. In fact, I had to be pretty careful what I told Mum, if I wanted to avoid this 'competing over who could be the most *over*-protective'.

It had been on the tip of my tongue that morning to tell her about the card. But in her current mood the idea of me doing a flat-by-flat search for missing persons unknown was hardly going to appeal. So I decided to keep the whole thing to myself. I went and ran a big hot bath – always the best place to think things over.

I lay in the water racking my brains for the right way to go about bringing my two unknown lovers together. Maybe I could put posters up on all the lampposts like people do for a lost cat.

MISSING
Jane
Please contact Henry
who desperately wants to hear from you

With my mobile number for further information. Then I imagined what Mum would say with all these weirdos calling me up. *Certainly* not a good idea. Or maybe I should contact the local radio station. I could imagine the DJ's voice:

'Hey Jane, if you're out there, this is your lucky day. Henry is longing to hear from you. He loves you, baby. Don't keep him waiting too long. I'll just put on a smoochie number to bring you two lovers together . . . '

But I could hardly count on Jane or Henry listening in, could I? Or maybe I should put out a message on the net.

From: Henry <HenryWhoever@
           compuserve.com>
To: JaneSeymour@lostinthepost4evR
Sent: 22 April 2002
Subject: ♥ng U

Will you marry me?

But if Henry had been into computers, instead of trusting the post, wouldn't he have e-mailed her? He hadn't, he'd sent a card. So *sweet* and old-fashioned and romantic of him. Poor Henry, wherever you are. You shouldn't be suffering like this.

I could picture him now, sitting by the phone, waiting for it to ring. Day in day out, night after night, *nothing*. And then maybe walking out across the common in desperation . . . getting to the bridge across the river . . . and pausing to stare down into the dark eddying water. He's about to throw himself in. Climbing up on to the ironwork of the bridge, edging his way along a girder. Just at that moment, he catches sight of Jane across the street. (Hey. There was a story here. Enough material for a whole blockbuster.) He's *slipped*. He's there clinging to a girder, but his fingers are losing their grip. Jane has caught sight of him, she's shading her eyes against the sun . . .

'How long are you going to be in there?' Mum's voice came through my reverie. 'Your boiled egg's as hard as rock and you've got to change Bag's kitty litter or it'll walk out of its own accord.'

(So much for romance!) 'Nearly finished. I'm out now.' The water had gone stone cold.

* * *

An hour or so later, I was making my way down the stairs to the bins with the rubbish bag. The lift wasn't working as usual. Just as I passed Jekyll and Hyde's front door, Jekyll shot out ahead of me. He stabbed at the lift button.

'It's jammed,' I informed him. He muttered something inaudible, then shot down the stairs two at a time. He was about the right height for Roz, I reckoned. But was he really father-material?

I was still musing about this when I reached the hallway. The front doors were thrust open and Cedric crashed through carrying his bike, dressed in full racing gear complete with helmet.

'Hi Jessica,' he gasped. He was red in the face and had big sweat marks on his T-shirt.

'You look hot,' I commented.

'Just done 50 k in under an hour and with a headwind,' he said.

'Re-ally!' I said, trying to sound suitably awestruck.

'Yeah well, phew,' he said and rested on his bike.

'Lift's stuck. I'll send it down for you if you hang on,' I said, turning to start my journey back up.

'No, wait . . . '

'What?'

He took his helmet off. His hair was plastered to the top of his head where the helmet had been, and the tidal wave stuck out beneath like a kind of horizontal halo. He was still trying desperately to get his breath back.

'What are doing later today?' he gasped.

I had been planning a really thorough floor-by-floor search for Jane, but there was no time like the present . . .

'Clare's coming over. We thought we might drop by on you. Hear some of your stuff?'

'Yeah? Great! I'll get some munchies in.'

'See you then.'

I ran up the next few flights and called Clare straightaway. 'Listen, Clare. Confirmation! You're on. He wants you to come round.' (A slight exaggeration, but it worked like magic.)

'Does he?'

'To listen to some of his stuff.'

'Really?' Her voice sounded doubtful.

'Rule one. Take an interest in his interests,' I reminded her.

'I have! He's already bored me rigid with his bike. And I don't know anything about . . . what's it called?'

'Jungle.'

'I don't even know what it *sounds* like.'

In the circumstances I thought it wouldn't be a bad idea to suss up on the key elements of the 'jungle' scene. I agreed to meet Clare in the high street at Virgin Megastore. The guy behind the counter was so laid-back he was scary.

I cleared my throat. 'Have you got any "jungle"?'

'What are you after, mainstream or alternative?'

I exchanged glances with Clare. 'Alternative,' she said.

'Nah, no call for it.'

'Mainstream, then?'

'Which artist in particular?'

(Tricky question.) 'What have you got?'

He reeled off a list of names that meant absolutely nothing to either of us. We had to get him to repeat it twice before we settled on a shortlist. Then we spent ages listening to bits on the headphones. The trouble was they all sounded the same. In the end we settled on a compilation CD with the nicest-looking guy on the cover.

Clare went home to do a two-hour 'jungle' crash-course, determined to get to like it.

* * *

By four that afternoon we were at Cedric's place. His mum was out so the coast was clear to play music as loud as we liked. He led us towards a door at the rear of the flat. Throwing it open, he showed us into his room.

I've seen lots of boy's rooms, mostly of the knee-deep in slowly composting clothes variety. But Cedric's room could get into the *Guinness Book of Records* for tidiness. The walls were lined with metal shelving units, packed so tight with sleeves that you could hardly fit a credit card between them.

'All vinyl,' he said proudly. 'All original recordings.'

'Where did you get them?' asked Clare.

'Specialists. White-label outlets.'

'Uh huh?' she said, raising an eyebrow at me. I shrugged. Neither of us had the faintest idea what he was talking about.

'Want to hear something?'

'You choose,' said Clare.

Cedric shifted a carefully stacked pile of music magazines and made a space for us to sit down. Then he took out a record from a sleeve, wiped it round with reverence, and put it on. A minute or so later the air was filled with some bloke blurting unintelligible lyrics against a backing of clashing saucepan lids. Clare was nodding her head like a noddy dog, in dutiful appreciation. I sat patiently through the first three tracks, then I reckoned the time had come for me to leave.

'That was *great*!' I said, getting to my feet. 'Look, I don't want to break things up, but I promised Mum I'd, errm, vacuum before she gets back.'

'But if you liked that, you've got to hear this,' said Cedric, reaching for another record. I sat through a further track.

'And this one's really brilliant,' he said, climbing on a chair to reach down another.

'But not as good as Slaphead Sam,' I heard Clare say.

'You like Slaphead?' said Cedric, his face lighting up. 'You're the first girl I've met who could really relate to Slap. I've got one of his early recordings somewhere.'

I looked at Clare in admiration. She'd certainly learned fast. Cedric was already thumbing through his racks. Clare was helping him.

'Jeez, you're organised,' she said. 'These are all in alphabetical order.' (Is that sad, or what?)

I looked on as Cedric took Clare on a guided tour

of his collection from A-Z. They were well into the Bs when I decided that they really truly didn't need me. So I piled it on about how incredibly urgent the vacuuming was, not to mention the dusting and washing-up, and made my escape.

I didn't get a total debrief on the 'jungle' session until next day when Clare and I met up on the bus. The cross-examination didn't go exactly the way I wanted.

'So, how was it?'

'Fine.'

'Has he made a move yet?'

'Not exactly.'

'Body language?'

'Not unless you count standing on my toe.'

'Not even a mini snog-ette?'

She shook her head. 'I don't know what I did wrong,' she complained. 'I kept kind of hinting. He could have asked me out.'

'Be patient. True love waits.'

'By the time Cedric gets round to it, I reckon true love will've given up and gone home.'

'Rubbish.'

Clare continued moaning all the way to school. And then it got worse. We were dumping our coats in the cloakroom when Christine arrived. She had a little flock of her fans in attendance. I raised my eyebrows at Clare in the mirror.

Christine set about putting on lip-gloss while talking nonstop to her awestruck audience. A feat that takes some doing. She was describing in minute detail what she was going to wear to the Cranshaw Ball.

The Cranshaw Memorial Ball was held by Cranshaw High – the private boys' school where her boyfriend Matt went. To receive an invitation to it was a real cornerstone of status in our school. And as it happened, it was Cedric's school too. I could see that Clare had overheard Christine.

'It's got shoestring straps and is really low-cut at the back . . .'

'It's a pretty cheesy affair . . . ' I whispered comfortingly.

Clare stared at me. 'Just because *you* haven't been invited.'

'And I'm going to wear those really shiny flesh-tone tights . . . ' Christine continued. 'With sling-backs and . . . '

'Nor have you . . . ' I whispered back.

Clare looked up with a hurt expression in her eyes. '*Yet.*'

Having finished the task of demoralising us by occupying the central position in the mirror and brushing her perfect fall of glossy blonde hair, so that it kind of *whooshed* all over us, Christine swept out of the cloakroom, leaving a scent of musk and sandalwood behind her.

Clare turned to me. 'He's *got* to invite me.'

I nodded. 'Sure thing. We'll have to put the pressure on.'

'How?'

'I don't know.'

'Think!'

'An image upgrade?'

'What's that?'

'New clothes, new make-up, *new image*.'

We agreed on an after-school shopping session the next day. I was determined that Clare wasn't going to settle for her favourite totally characterless beige. However, despite my protests, she managed to lure me into Gap.

We were sharing a cubicle while Clare tried to decide which of the six different cuts of chinos was the most flattering. The pair she had on squeezed her in at the hips so that a little rim of superfluous Clare bulged over the top. Catching her reflection at an unfortunate angle, she said in a kind of broken voice, 'I know what the problem is. It's because I'm fat, isn't it?'

'No way!' I said. But I don't think I sounded very convincing. She'd caught me off my guard. I mean, Clare is kind of rounded in places where I'm not, which could be seen as an advantage. No, let's face it, to be honest, she could do with shedding a few pounds.

'You're lovely,' I tried reassuring her. 'You've got incredible skin . . . ' (I could hear myself saying it – skin is like the meagrest of compliments) ' . . . and wonderful eyes and hair to die for. If Cedric can't see that he must be blind.'

But Clare was insistent. She was skewing herself round so she could see her entire back view. 'Look!' she said. 'Check it out. You see all that there? That's cellulite.' Her eyes were brimming now. 'I'm gross. I know it.'

'That is just *so* untrue.'

But Clare was adamant. She was groping for her clothes and dragging them on blindly. 'That's it. I'm going on a diet. I'm not going to eat another thing until I'm like – ten pounds lighter.'

'Look, Clare, that's mad. You don't need to diet. Just cut out something like, say – chocolate.'

'There, you've admitted it. You *do* think I'm fat.'

'No. No way. I don't!'

The Gap girl chose that unfortunate moment to intervene. She had just taken a breath and was about to come out with her standard patter of how great Clare looked in her chinos – you know, '*retail reassurance*', all that '*confirming your choice*' stuff – when Clare stuffed a waving sea of beige legs into her arms.

'Is everything all right?'

Clare looked the Gap girl up and down – she was a tactlessly perfect size eight.

'You wouldn't understand,' said Clare, and stormed out of the shop.

chapter seven

It was on the way back from the high street in the bus, when I was sifting through my backpack trying to locate my bus pass, that I came across the purple envelope again. Ooops! It made me feel *really* guilty. With all this involvement in Cedric = Clare, I had totally forgotten about Jane + Henry.

I walked back to Rosemount wondering what they were each doing right now. Jane, I decided, would be sitting at her window, gazing into the sunset wondering why she hadn't heard from Henry. And Henry . . . Maybe he was taking Jane's picture out of his wallet, gazing at it sadly, deciding to tear it up and try to forget her.

The late evening sun was shining on Rosemount, making it look incredibly romantic in spite of its shabbiness. It was so frustrating. The key to finding Jane *must* be somewhere inside. I hadn't checked the ground floor yet – flat number one. It belonged to an M. Zamoyski or Madame Zamoyski as I'd christened her – the *clairvoyant*.

In the gathering dusk her flat looked dark and kind of spooky from the outside. Behind the nets the heavy curtains were almost completely drawn but there was a slight glow inside as if there was a light on low. As I put my finger on her bell I felt a tingle of nerves. The hairs on the back of my neck were standing on end. This was ridiculous. It was all my imagination – the whole thing about her being a clairvoyant I mean – and partly a joke.

I paused for a moment and then drew a deep breath and rang firmly. I could hear the ringing sound reverberating within. I waited a few moments. Then I heard shuffling footsteps. The door opened. In the half-light, I could see a small, well-rounded woman, her grey hair drawn back into a very clairvoyantish bun and fastened at the sides by two tortoiseshell combs.

'Yes, my dear? Can I help you?' Her accent was middle-European.

'I just wondered . . . ' My voice faltered as beyond her, in the deep gloom of the room, I caught sight of a round table set with a baize cloth and illuminated by a low-hanging lamp with a leaded glass shade. The dull heavy ticking of a cabinet clock added to the spooky atmosphere.

'Yes?'

Could I distinguish a slight sulphuric smell in the air? Ether? A whiff of decomposition brought over from the spirit world?

'I just wondered if you knew of anyone by the name of Seymour, who lives or may have lived here?' It all came out in a rush.

'Seymour?' she said thoughtfully, with her head cocked on one side. 'I think there were some Seymours here once. Maybe, if you have a moment, I could see if I could call them up for you. Come in my dear.'

(*Call them up?*) I glanced at the table and shivered. (I don't believe in ghosts or spirits, *no way*. But unfortunately that doesn't stop you being scared of them.)

'Come and sit down,' said Madame Zamoyski, beckoning me into the room.

Two thin fingers of late evening sun fell across a grand piano which was stacked with dusty sepia photos of people long dead. The rest of the room was in the deepest shadow.

'Oh, no, really. I can't stop.'

'I am expecting company, but there's no one due here for a good half hour.'

'But . . . '

'It won't take a minute . . . ' She took a key and started to unlock a roll-top desk. There was a sudden shrill buzzing from the further room that made me almost jump out of my skin.

'Oh dear, there you go. Hold on a second. I'll be with you in a minute.' She slipped behind a beaded curtain and disappeared from sight.

From beyond the curtain came a strange hollow tapping sound. The sulphuric smell *grew stronger* . . .

I stared after her. The bead curtain quivered, as if some vapour from the afterworld was disturbing the air. At any moment I could envisage some spectral figure coming through. I got to my feet, my knees feeling totally weak. Calling out something to the effect that I would drop by again, I escaped from the flat shutting her door firmly behind me.

I ran up the stairs as fast as I could with my heart pounding – and bumped slap bang into Cedric.

'Hold it. What's the hurry? What were you doing at Mrs Z's?'

'Long story.'

'You look in a state. What's up?'

'Shhh!' We peered over the bannisters. Some people had let themselves in silently through the main front door. Three figures in dark coats were now standing outside Madame Zamoyski's flat. We heard the echoing ring of her doorbell, and then she ushered them in. The door clicked shut after them.

'Do you realise what she's doing down there?' I whispered.

'What?'

'She's having a seance.' I explained about the round table and the smell of sulphur. 'I bet they're in there now, hands linked, calling up the dead.'

Cedric snorted with laughter. 'Monday is Mrs Z's bridge afternoon.'

'But her flat, everything. She looks just like a clairvoyant.'

'Mrs Z? No way!'

'So what about the smell of sulphur?'

'Probably her egg-and-cress bridge rolls,' said Cedric dismissively. 'What were you doing in her place, anyway?'

I hesitated. I'd promised myself I wouldn't tell anyone. But Cedric was so harmless he didn't really count. And I didn't have to tell him the whole story. So I started. 'If you were sent a letter. Say an anonymous letter from someone. And you wanted to track them down. What would you do?'

'An anonymous letter?'

'Well, kind of. A letter from someone who didn't give their address.'

'First thing I'd do is check the postmark. Every postmark shows when and where a letter was posted.'

'Cedric, you know what? You're brilliant!' I leaned over the bannisters and spontaneously, totally without thinking, gave him a big smacker on the cheek.

He blushed scarlet. 'Look, Jessica, if you want to talk about it . . . I mean, an anonymous letter. If you need any help . . . '

'No, it's OK, it's nothing like that. I've got to go.' I raced up the last flight of stairs to our flat, raked out the card again and studied it more closely.

There was the postmark. 7-4-02 Forest Vale. Lower down, a little hard to decipher, were some letters and numbers.

How stupid of me. I'd been spending all my time looking for Jane. What I should have been doing was searching for Henry.

I hid the card away at the bottom of my sock drawer and thought hard about how to go about it.

chapter eight

Forest Vale. I was used to seeing the name on my bus every day, written up over the driver. It was the last stop on the 74 bus route – the one that went back and forth to our school. I'd always pictured it as having loads of tall pine trees with a shady river running up through them. And little grassy clearings. The kind of place you could go to with friends and have a really cool picnic.

So the following Saturday afternoon, since I didn't have much on, I decided to take a trip down there and check it out. Dad was going to pick up the Harley, so he'd cancelled our usual afternoon together. I told Mum I was going to do some research for my geography project. I even sorted out a clipboard to take with me to look convincing.

I gazed happily out of the window as the bus idled its way through the Saturday morning traffic. I was sure that I'd find Henry in Forest Vale. It couldn't be too difficult – in a place like that. It would just be a matter of asking around.

Streets full of busy shoppers passed in a kind of daze as I sat daydreaming that I'd actually found Henry and brought him and Jane together. I was at their wedding and Henry was presenting a special toast to me. It was at this really gorgeous house, with massive columns at the front and a park with deer in it. I was chief bridesmaid and was wearing this totally amazing dress – pure silk and floaty, kind of like the dress Gwyneth Paltrow wore in *Shakespeare in Love*. And Dad and Mum had been invited to the wedding as well. They were standing together holding hands and raising their glasses . . . When the bus drew to a juddering stop.

'Forest Vale,' called out the driver. 'All change.'

The other passengers were already standing in the aisle ready to get off. This was the end of the route. I stared out of the window in disbelief. This was no leafy vale. There wasn't a tree in sight. There was nothing but acres of concrete leading up to a brand new shopping mall. The driver had vacated his cab and stood eyeing me. I was the only person left on the bus.

'All change,' he repeated. I got off and watched as

he made his way over to a café called 'Muggins' which had a row of jolly mugs with faces painted on them displayed in the window.

I was at a total loss as to how to start my search. How could I tell if Henry lived here or not? There wasn't a house in sight. I made for the mall anyway. Hey, there were some quite cool shops inside. Before I knew it I was deep into an intensive window-shop. I was even tempted into one or two boutiques and had tried on three summer tops, five pairs of trainers and some rather dodgy bell-bottoms before I came face to face with a post office. Which reminded me why I was in Forest Vale in the first place. I was meant to be looking for Henry, wasn't I?

I pushed open the door and found a long row of people patiently queueing in a roped-off area. The post people themselves were protected from their customers by a security glass window. You weren't allowed to get to them until a bossy electronic voice told you which window was free. Everyone ahead of me seemed to be relicensing cars, or applying for pensions or doing something that took for ever. I stood there reading the various excruciatingly boring post office notices while an impatient shuffling queue built up behind me.

Thankfully at that point my mobile rang.

'Hi! Where are you?' It was Clare.

'Errm . . . ' I didn't exactly feel like explaining to her that I was in a post office queue on some sad, mad, wild goose chase for a guy I didn't even know, so I countered with, 'Where are you?'

It worked. 'Don't ask! I've been sitting here for an hour and a half and I've drunk three cappuccinos and it's cost a bomb and—'

'You're in Costa's?'

'Errm. I just thought. I mean, you did say Cedric hung out here.'

'Did I?'

'Yes.'

I thought fast. 'Look, you're probably too early. Stay where you are. He could well turn up.'

'You really think so?'

'Yes.'

I hung up and called Cedric straightaway. 'Hi. How's things. What are you up to?'

'Right now?'

'Mmm.'

'Making up a catalogue on my laptop. Means I should be able to locate any track within—'

(Was that sad or what?) 'Listen,' I interrupted. 'Do you fancy a coffee?'

'Sure, I'll be right up.'

'No . . . listen, I'm not at home. I'm at Costa's. You know, the new coffee bar in the high street.'

'Right. When?'

'Soon as you can make it.'

'Well, I guess I could finish this later . . . '

'Great!'

At that point the electronic voice announced: *'Cashier number six, please.'*

'What's that?' asked Cedric.

'My mobile's playing up,' I said, and rang off. When I reached the counter my particular post person was a female. 'Can I help you?' she asked.

Painfully aware that mine was a totally ridiculous request, I took the card out of my bag and passed it through the opening in her window. 'Please could you tell me whether or not this card was posted here?'

She held the postmark under her lamp and then confirmed that it was indeed posted in a postbox in the 'vicinity'.

'Do you know which one?'

She frowned and disappeared into the back, returning with a ledger. After huffing and faffing and running her finger down several columns she announced that the box in question was on the out-skirts of the precinct, and gave me directions as to how to find it.

Searching my way through the maze of brightly lit shops, I at last emerged from the mall and tracked down box GRNWD 34X standing like a lone red dalek in a corner of a windblown square.

I'd found it. Brilliant!

I loitered beside it. There wasn't a soul in sight. There was nothing in the square apart from an overfilled rubbish bin, a lamppost and a stark concrete bench. But there was a street that led off it which looked more hopeful. It was flanked by rows of brand new town houses. There was not a move-ment in any of them. No one walked their dog. There wasn't even a stray cat. I went back to the square and sat down on the bench. This was really depressing. As squares go this one must be the most boring one in Britain. Short of taking up residence beside the postbox and cross-questioning every male that came within a certain radius, I was no further on.

That's when my mobile rang again. It was Clare. 'He still hasn't turned up.'

'Hasn't he?'

'I think I'll go home now.'

'No don't . . . I mean another ten minutes or so won't make any difference.'

No sooner had I rung off than I had Cedric on the line. 'Where are you?' he asked.

'Where are you?'

'At Costa's. And you're not.'

'You can't be.'

'What do you mean?'

'Errm, isn't anyone else there?' I asked. (What on earth had happened to Clare?)

'Loads of people.'

'Look, wait right there. OK?'

I rang Clare again. 'Where are you?'

'I left. I was feeling really stupid sitting all on my own.'

'But he's there now. Go back.'

'How do you know?' she asked.

(Tricky question.) 'Look, do as I say. I just know, OK?' I rang off. I stared at the phone. Oh well, I guessed they'd sort themselves out somehow.

But what about Henry? I took the envelope out of my bag and stared at it for inspiration. If this were a true forensic investigation the handwriting would be a key issue. There was something oddly familiar about it. But maybe I'd looked at it so many times it had kind of imprinted itself on my memory. It was black, written, I reckoned, with a medium roller ball, which narrowed down the possible users to around half the population of the developed world.

But I still had the card to go on. It was more than likely bought in the mall. I made my way back inside and soon spotted a shop which sold gift wrap and greetings cards. It had rack upon rack of cards for every occasion. I worked my way through hazy landscapes and cartoon cats, bald men with jokey speech bubbles, fawning teddy bears, pipes and golf clubs and vintage cars, right down to cards with 'Congratulations on passing your driving test' before I found a section entitled: 'No message'. There, squashed under a random selection of fat ladies, I found it. Exactly the same card: 'To someone special'. I was so surprised that I actually took the card up to the counter and bought it.

The girl at the check-out had been giving me evil glances while I was shuffling through her display racks (and I wasn't making them *that* untidy). 'Found what you were looking for, then?' she asked.

I nodded. She didn't look as if she was in a helpful mood, but I asked anyway, 'You wouldn't happen to remember who last bought a card like this, would you?'

She looked at me as if I'd gone stark raving bonkers. 'If I could remember everyone who bought a card in this shop, I'd be doing something better than working here, I can tell you.'

'Yes, well, that's what I thought. Thanks anyway.'

I then concentrated my attention on her roller balls and, while she had her back turned, I surreptitiously tested several black ones against Henry's handwriting. The third was a perfect match. So I bought that too.

I retraced my steps to the postbox (still no one there). It was at that point that my mobile rang again.

It was Cedric. 'You did say the *new* place in the high street?'

'Yes!'

'The one in the bookshop?'

'In the bookshop? No. That's not Costa's.'

'That explains it then. Why you're not here.'

'Yes, I suppose it does,' I said weakly, and rang off.

I rang Clare. 'Look, I've had an idea. If he's not in Costa's, why don't you try the new coffee shop in Bookfest?'

'If I drink another coffee I'll puke,' said Clare. 'I'm

going home.' And she rang off. She sounded really fed up.

I sank down on the bench again. It had turned into a nightmare of a day. And I was still no further on with my search for Henry. My eye rested on the pub sign opposite. 'The Jolly Sailor.' The sailor on the sign was grinning at me most unsympathetically. I put my tongue out at him.

But why hadn't I thought of it before? Pubs were the haunt of single males, weren't they? I'm tall for my age and could easily get away with going into a bar alone. I made my way across to it. I pushed open the door and paused. That was odd. There was a poster on the wall for The Lansdowne Players – in fact, for the play Mum was in, *'Eight into Six Won't Go' by George Williams*. They were certainly doing a lot of publicity.

I forged my way into the haze of smoke and stale beer. The room was crowded with blokes, any one of whom could have been Henry. I made my way over to the bar, trying to look as tall and confident as possible. I ordered a Coke and a packet of crisps. The barman looked at me suspiciously but didn't ask for ID.

'Will that be all, Miss?'

'Erm . . . I just wondered if you knew of anyone called Henry who comes in here?'

'Henry who?'

'I don't know his surname.'

'What's he look like?'

'I don't know.'

'What age?'

I shook my head again.

'Bit of a mystery man, eh?'

'I know he's single,' I said.

'Blind date, is it?'

'Kind of.'

He gazed at me, polishing a glass as he did so. 'Henry . . . Henry . . . ' he said, racking his brain. He turned to the crowd of drinkers. 'Young lady here is looking for a bloke called Henry?'

This was greeted by a load of guffawing and and offers. But when they'd calmed down they helpfully suggested possibilities. There was Henry Jones who turned out to be in his nineties. Henry Wilson, but he'd moved. At last, we wittled them down to a Henry who sounded a likely candidate. He was young, single and local, and studying something to do with film lighting at tech – pretty cool. The man was just writing the address for me on my clipboard, when I heard the bar door swing open behind me.

A horribly familiar voice exclaimed, 'Jessica Mayhew. *What* are *you* doing here?'

I nearly jumped out of my skin. I swung round. It was Mr Williams, of all people. He was looking at me as if I was a delinquent. He obviously had the impression that I generally spent my time hanging around in bars.

'Mr Williams . . . hello. What are you doing here?'

'This is my local. I live round here. But I didn't expect to find one of my students in it.'

I stared into my Coke. He was bound to tell Mum. 'Please, Mr Williams, I can explain everything.'

'Explain away, Jessica.'

'You see, it's for my geography project,' I started, indicating my clipboard.

He didn't look convinced. 'A geography project in a pub?'

'It's a study of forenames in the outer city suburbs,' I explained. 'You won't tell my mother I was in here, will you?'

He raised an eyebrow. 'I think maybe we could keep this between ourselves. As long as it doesn't happen again.'

'Oh, it won't.'

'Want another Coke?'

'No thanks.'

'OK, I'm going into town. I'll give you a lift.'

chapter nine

When we arrived at Rosemount Mr Williams said, 'Is your mother in?'

I looked up. I could see the tell-tale light shining through our front window. The last thing I wanted was for him to come up and to have to explain everything.

'No, I don't think so,' I lied.

'Well, go straight up then,' he said.

'Yes, Mr Williams. Thanks for the lift.'

I found Mum spread out on the kitchen table with her laptop plugged into the kettle socket. Which meant a cup of tea was out of the question. Obviously, she was deep into one of her OU essays. The kitchen looked ominously food-free.

'Where've you been?'

'Doing research for my geography project.'

'Oh yes, of course, I forgot.'

'What's for supper?'

'Supper? Oh . . . What's the time?'

'Seven-thirty.'

'Oh dear. I had this deadline . . . '

'Which means that you forgot to shop.'

'Maybe you could pop out and . . . '

'Too late.'

'The deli's open.'

'They charge a fortune.'

'There are some eggs, I think.'

'OK, that'll do. I'll make us an omelette.'

I slopped around with eggs and the whisk while Mum tapped away frantically at her keyboard. It wasn't fair. Other people's mums made meals. In the old days, before she went out to work, she used to do her essays during the day. Now, what with her job and her OU course and her drama group, I was lucky if I got fed at all. If only we could be a proper family again.

I glanced at Mum. She was wearing that saggy cardie as usual. And those terrible leggings. And her glasses had slipped down on her nose. Love goddess NOT. Perhaps I could get her to stop wearing her specs. She didn't really need them. Well, perhaps for reading. But she could see perfectly well without them for most things. And once the specs were off I could maybe get her to use some eye make-up. She had nice eyes – she ought to make the most of them.

It was parents' evening at school the coming Thursday. And it occurred to me that it was the one time when Mum and Dad actually had to meet up. This would be a good opportunity to raise Mum's profile in Dad's eyes. But how? Should I burn the saggy cardie? Could I force her into heels?

I decided to try the slow drip-feed brain-washing approach. While clearing up the meal later that night, I mentioned, 'You know it's parent-teacher night on Thursday?'

'Is it? Again?'

'I put it in your diary.' She was getting incredibly forgetful these days.

'Oh right. Better remind your father.'

'I already have.'

There was a pause while she filled the washing-up bowl with new water.

'What were you thinking of wearing?' I asked.

'No idea. Why?'

'It'd be nice if you could look nice, that's all.'

'Can't you think of a more inspired adjective?'

'Well, other people's mothers make an effort.'

'I'll think about it.'

* * *

On Monday I happened to be taking a short cut home through Braithwaites, our local department store, when I was approached by a girl handing out leaflets for a 'Free Skincare and Make-up Consultation'. They were giving away a load of cosmetics if you took it up. And it was a really expensive brand. Cool! I headed over to the counter to check it out.

Under a banner saying: 'Colour your World', a woman in a crisp white overall had a customer pinned down on a swivel chair. I hovered. She was going the whole hog with the blusher . . .

As she turned to load her brush with more powder she caught sight of me. 'Can I help you?'

Suddenly, I was terribly aware of standing there in my school uniform. The whole place felt all glossy and perfumy and her counter was covered with photos of perfectly made-up models who all seemed to be staring disdainfully at me – in fact, straight at my shiny nose. I could feel my open pores gaping like craters.

'Umm . . . could I book a consultation, please?'

'I'll be with you in a minute,' she said with a frown. She returned to her client and started telling her how wonderful she looked. The lady who'd been given the make-over seemed really pleased with the end result – at any rate, she was flourishing her credit card. I watched as a carrier was filled with mega-bucks worth of glossy packages.

The consultant then set about tidying up her brushes, totally ignoring me. I think she hoped I was going to give up and walk away, which was under-standable. Currently dressed, I didn't look like the kind of person she'd want to have associated with her brand.

I coughed politely.

'So what can I do for you?' she said with a forced smile.

'I'd like a consultation, please.'

'I really don't know if I can fit you in.'

'It's not for me. It's for my mother.'

This seemed to have a reassuring effect on her. 'Oh, that's nice. Surprise treat, is it?'

'Kind of.'

She brought out her appointments book. After a bit of haggling about times. I managed to book Mum in for the last session of the actual day on which we were due to have our parent-teacher meeting. Nice one.

*   *   *

I thought I'd be up against some resistance when I mentioned the make-over to Mum.

'Thursday. But that's the night we've got to be at school,' she pointed out.

'It's late night shopping at Braithwaites. You've got time for the make-over first.'

'Oh yes, I suppose I have,' she said, looking vague. And then she smiled. 'Why not?'

That Thursday evening when I got home from school, I found Mum had made an effort. She'd put on her new cream polo sweater and her one pair of trousers that actually fitted, with boots that had enough heel to give her some height. She came to look at her reflection in the long hall mirror. She'd had a haircut that day and her hair was all smooth and blow-dried and shiny. In fact, she looked pretty good.

'Oh, I don't really want to bother with this stupid make-over,' she said.

'But you have to. I've booked it. Look, it says you have to ring to cancel the appointment. It's too late now.' I wasn't going to let her back out while I was doing so well.

So we drove to Braithwaites. I practically frog-marched her to the make-over counter. The consultation started with a question and answer session. Mum kept on giving me these 'looks' over the woman's shoulder. It seemed Mum didn't cleanse, she didn't tone and she'd never used a night cream. The woman seemed surprised that Mum still had a *face*. When it came to 'analysing your make-up routine' it was even more humiliating. Mum had no idea of her skin type, she didn't know what her skin tone was and she'd last bought a lipstick five years ago.

The woman sighed in disbelief and tied a kind of white plastic bib thing round Mum's neck. I reckoned she should have been pleased. Mum was positively virgin territory as far as a make-over was concerned.

Anyway, Mum gave the consultant a free hand. Actually, she didn't have much alternative because she had to take her glasses off, so she couldn't see what the woman was up to.

I watched in silence as Mum's familiar features disappeared and were gradually replaced by a stranger's mask. Her eyelashes were standing out individually like spider legs and her lips were so glossy they looked as if they'd slid out of *Hello!* magazine. I looked at her doubtfully. Was this the kind of look men went for? Or, more importantly, was it going to impress Dad?

'There you go,' said the consultant and whipped the bib off. She seemed satisfied with the result. She started reeling off a list of compliments. Admittedly they sounded a bit like what she'd said to the other woman. Mum nodded vaguely and groped in her handbag for her glasses. As usual, she couldn't locate them.

At that moment a bell went off to announce that Braithwaites was about to close. This was the cue for the make-over woman to go into a high-speed, hard-sell on all the products she'd used. Mum tentatively enquired as to the price of a lipstick. Her eyes met mine in horror when she heard the answer. She backed down hurriedly to a kohl eye pencil and was about to fork out for that when luckily we ran out of time.

The counters were being covered with dust-cloths. So we managed to escape with our tiny gift bag of free cosmetics, containing, I established later, round about enough to make up a very small mouse.

'I had no idea a lipstick could cost that much,' said Mum when we were back in the car, heading towards school.

'It's a very good brand.'

'It must be. But fancy paying that for a *lipstick*.

Anyway, what are we talking about? I don't wear lipstick.'

'Maybe you should,' I said meaningfully.

We'd stopped at some lights. Mum had at last located her glasses and she swivelled the rear view mirror so that she could take a look at herself.

'Oh my God!' she said. 'Jessica, how could you let her do this to me? What *do* I look like?'

'You look fine. You look great.'

She was groping in her bag for a tissue.

'Leave it. You'll smudge everything.'

We continued on our way with Mum grumbling and moaning.

'What does it matter anyway,' I said. 'It's only school.'

As we parked in the school car park there was an explosive farty noise behind us. O-m-G. It was Dad on his new Harley.

He climbed off. He was dressed from head to foot in biker's black leatherwear – he even had on one of those round retro cycle helmets. He raised a hand in greeting. He looked just like a Michelin man in negative.

Mum didn't recognise him for a moment. And then as he approached she muttered, 'Oh my goodness, it's your father. What does he think he looks like?'

'It's for the bike,' I said.

'I should think it is.' Mum eyed the bike in silent hostility. Dad turned and gave it an affectionate pat as if it were a horse or something. 'Fancy coming to a parents' evening dressed like that,' said Mum in an undertone.

Things weren't going at all the way I'd planned. I had one parent looking really good, i.e. Mum après make-over plus cream sweater plus nice trousers . . . And the other one looking like an overweight biker-boy. I mean, I wished Mum had never made the effort. Now they were even more out of balance than ever.

M + (amo + cs + nt) > D + (ow bb)
Mega Mismatch

Dad unstrapped the helmet. I could tell he thought he looked really cool. But actually he was red in the face and his hair was all over the place.

'Hello there,' he said, rapidly taking in Mum's new glossy image. 'You're looking, er . . . *well*.'

He was impressed. I could tell. He hadn't seen

Mum looking like that for years. In fact, not ever. There was that awful pause when any normal couple would have given each other a peck on the cheek. Ever since they'd broken up they always looked as if they were about to – and then didn't.

'Umm, we'd better hurry,' I said, to break the ice. 'It's nearly seven-thirty.'

'Sure thing. Hello, Poppet,' he said, giving me a hug. 'Better find out what you've been up to, eh?'

Inside the school, the hall was seething with parents. The teachers had set themselves up behind desks armed with loose-leaf files full of lists of marks. I used my usual tactic which was to steer Mum and Dad to the teachers whose subjects I was best at, while they were fully focused. We could deal with things like maths and chemistry later on when their attention was waning.

So we started with Mr Williams. I was a bit worried about the Forest Vale encounter. I mean, Mr Williams said he wouldn't tell, but you could never totally rely on adults when they got together. But he seemed to have his thoughts elsewhere. He took one look at Mum and did a double-take. I must admit, under the bright school lights she did look rather like a Barbie doll.

He hurriedly glanced back at his file notes and started running a pen down his list of marks. He seemed unusually flustered. His eyes kept resting uneasily on Dad's leatherwear. I felt really embarrassed. I mean, most people's fathers had come straight from work and were in suits and things. Dad looked as if he was about to produce a bike chain out of his pocket and attack someone. All this was bound to confirm in Mr Williams's mind that I was a total drop out. No wonder I hung around in bars.

Mr Williams cleared his throat. 'Ah, Jessica. Now, let's see. Hmm.' And then he had the cheek to say that my term's average was somewhat disappointing. It worked out at a D. A *D*? I never get a D for English. English is my best subject.

'But I thought I'd get at least a B, Mr Williams.'

'Well, I was rather surprised. Now, what happened? Umm, yes. I think it was the *Pygmalion* coursework that brought your average down,' he said.

'But Mr Williams, I was really proud of that essay.'

'What was wrong with it?' asked Dad supportively.

Mr Williams shuffled through his papers and brought out some pages that I recognised as my essay. There was an awful lot of his red ink writing down the side.

'Uh huh. Yes. You were asked to comment on the relationship between Professor Higgins and Eliza . . .' he started.

'Which I did,' I protested. 'Anyone could see that Eliza and Professor Higgins should end up married in the end. They were like *made* for each other . . . '

'So why don't you think Bernard Shaw ended the play that way?' asked Mr Williams.

'I don't know. I think he got it wrong. The offer to teach her to talk properly and everything was just because the guy *fancied her like mad*. The elocution lessons were quite obviously an excuse. He just wanted her to stay over at his place . . . '

'Don't you think that maybe Shaw was making more of a social comment?'

'But my ending's so much better,' I protested.

Mr Williams sighed. '"*Eliza, be a doll*" – it's hardly Bernard Shaw now, is it?'

I could see Mum's chin wobble, the way it did when she was about to crack up. Her eyes briefly met Mr Williams's. Hang on. This was not in the least funny. That mark was going towards my GCSE coursework. I pointed this out. Dad agreed with me. In fact, he got to his feet and leaned somewhat threateningly towards Mr Williams.

Mr Williams started to gather his papers together and closed his file. He muttered something about not being able to enter into a discussion over coursework marks at an open evening. In fact, he seemed in a hurry to get rid of us. He called the next family up to his desk so we had to move on.

'That was so unfair,' I said to Mum.

'He is your teacher, Jessica.'

'Sounded like Jess had an interesting point to make . . . ' said Dad.

'But that's not what she was asked to do. The idea of literary criticism—' started Mum.

'You're taking his side then?' interrupted Dad.

'I'm not taking anyone's side. You haven't even read the play . . . '

Suddenly they were back into row mode. This wasn't how the evening was meant to turn out at all.

I steered them over to the history teacher. 'You're still two assignments behind, Jessica.'

Mum and Dad looked on while I tried to explain that it was merely a problem of time. I mean, history is such a *long* subject. The homework goes on for ever. And it always comes on Thursdays. Don't the teachers know about Thursdays? It's the one night-mare evening of the week because they all want assignments back on Friday to mark over the week-end. It's as if they each think their subject is the only one. What do they do in that staffroom of theirs? Don't they ever talk to each other?

The geography teacher had no better news.

'Six extensions this term, Jessica. It's just not good enough.'

I won't go into what happened further down the line of subjects. As we left the hall Dad and Mum were in a deep whispered discussion over whose fault it was that my marks had slipped. Predictably, they each blamed the other. As if I couldn't take credit for my poor averages all by myself.

chapter ten

Back at home Mum rushed to the bathroom and scrubbed her face. She looked out through the door with eye make-up running down her cheeks.

'That was the most embarrassing evening of my life,' she said. 'This stuff doesn't even come off with soap!'

I went and found her some of my waterproof mascara remover. 'I could see Dad thought you looked pretty good.'

'Your dad wasn't the only person there.'

'Apart from the other parents who you've known for years, and the teachers who don't matter.'

'What *did* your father *look* like?' she said, scrubbing vigorously at her eyes with a cotton-wool pad.

'Black leather is pretty cool.'

'He looked like a Hell's Angel. An ageing one. Pathetic, if you ask me. And look at your term's averages.'

'There's been a lot going on.'

'Too much. I think from now on, it would be a good idea if you stayed in more and concentrated on your homework, Jessica.'

'But I *am* concentrating. It's just that no one sees things the way I do.'

'The trouble with you is that you've too much imagination.'

'Isn't that meant to be a good thing?'

'Not if it's interfering with your work.'

I stared at her resentfully. She'd see things differently when I was a famous writer. The kind of person she studied in her OU set books. She'd be proud of me then.

'You don't understand. I've had a lot on my mind recently,' I complained.

Her face softened. 'Yes, I suppose you have. Like moving home and everything.'

I nodded. I hated fighting with Mum.

'Come on, let's have supper and a video. It's too late to do any homework tonight.'

We finished the evening eating spaghetti in front of a video of *The Bridges of Madison County*. It was one of Mum's favourites – she'd nearly worn out the copy from the video shop. It always made her cry.

'I don't know why you watch it,' I said as she reached for the tissue box.

'Nor do I,' she said, half-laughing and drying her eyes.

'I suppose it's nice to think people can still fall in love when they're old and everything.'

'They weren't old.'

'Clint Eastwood was all wrinkly and had grey hair.'

'So? Grey hair doesn't stop people being in love.'

'Doesn't it?'

'Of course not. It's the more important things that matter.'

'Like what?'

'All sorts of things. Liking the same people. Wanting to do the same things. Sharing the same interests . . . '

'What sort of interests?'

'Oh I don't know . . . Films and music and books and things . . . '

This got me thinking. One of Mum's constant moans was that Dad never read a decent book. So, that Saturday, instead of our usual meeting in the park, I'd suggested to Dad that we met up at Bookfest – our local bookshop, the one with the coffee bar which Cedric had mixed up with Costa's.

* * *

Bookfest was halfway up the high street. To get to it you had to go over the bridge that crossed the river. I decided to walk because I always loved to see the river – steel-grey in winter, all silver and glittery in summer, or like today, in spring, a sleek olive grey-green that slid beneath me as I paused midway across.

It was the first really warm day of the year. The river was gleaming in the sunlight. In the distance bright sailing boats were darting to and fro. Along the riverside, couples were walking hand in hand. Families with kids in pushchairs were heading for the play area in the park. I paused to watch a pleasure boat as it set sail from the pier. Happy couples leaned on the rails as they embarked on their journey upstream to the botanical gardens . . .

Which made me think of Clare and Cedric. Happy couple NOT. What they needed was some quality time alone together. That last time I'd tried to set them up had been such a disaster.

I watched the boat getting smaller and smaller as it steamed away. Which gave me an idea. Anyone on board would be trapped for an hour and a half with no way of escape. Water lapping by. There's nothing like water to bring on romance.

I made my way down the ramp to the timetable. There was another trip upstream at 4 p.m. Perfect! I texted Clare first.

dear wobble
love beckons
4pm boat upstream to Kew
be there or be dead
love j

Then I texted Cedric.

fancy a magical mystery tour?
4pm boat upstream to kew!
j

Then I made my way on up to the high street, happily imagining them meeting. Each surprised to see the other. They'd be looking out for me, of course, but when I didn't turn up it would be too late. The boat would be pulling out from the jetty and they'd both say they were sorry I'd missed it, but secretly they'd be glad to be on their own.

* * *

As usual, Dad was late, so I started browsing through the 'Three for Two' offers. These were mainly novels – always an uphill job to get him to read one of those. I lingered over a few war books and then headed for the non-fiction shelves.

Here was a netherworld of gardening books and DIY manuals, hardly qualifying for what Mum would call a 'good read'. I went back to the novels and searched through the titles. And then I spotted what seemed to be the perfect book. *Zen and the Art of Motorcycle Maintenance*. The Zen bit would appeal to Mum and it sounded as if it might be a handy book to help Dad with the new bike.

I paid for the book and went and sat at one of the coffee tables waiting for Dad. In a corner of the children's section a lady was sitting reading to a semi-circle of noisy toddlers. The toddlers weren't listening and I could see her getting hot and bothered behind her reading glasses as she tried unsuccessfully to win their attention without sounding cross.

Eventually, I spotted Dad coming through the doors. He was wearing a brand new jumper.

'Hey. You look good. Like the jumper. Who chose it?

He hesitated. 'Aren't I able to choose a jumper for myself?'

'Not without "go faster" stripes. No.'

'So just maybe I'm learning.'

'It must be my brainwashing.'

'That's right – clever you.' He changed the subject. 'What's that you've got there?'

'Birthday present.'

'For me?'

'Who else?'

'Well, thank you. Can I open it now?'

'Of course.'

'Ah! Ah ha! A book!' I could tell Dad was trying to sound pleased. 'Looks interesting.'

'Thought seeing as you'd bought the bike . . . '

'Nice one! Yeah, it looks . . . interesting,' he repeated.

'What do you want to do now?'

'How about a coffee and a browse?'

When our coffee came Dad took a little pack of artificial sweeteners out of his pocket.

'What's that for?'

He patted his stomach. 'Thought I'd try and fight back against anno Domini. I joined that gym, by the way.'

'Really? Good for you.'

'Your suggestion. Turned out to be one of the best things I've ever done.'

(Huh – so you see, you *can* influence people.)

When we'd finished our coffee Dad suggested a walk in the park. 'Then I thought I'd do us lunch at my place.'

'*You* cook lunch?'

'Well, maybe not cook, exactly.' He indicated a couple of supermarket bags he had with him. 'Put it together, maybe.'

'Cool.'

Dad hardly ever had me back to his place. I think he was a bit ashamed of it. He'd bought a flat in a really run-down estate. He'd wanted a two-bedroom one so that I could stay with him, and got it cheap. But I'd never actually stayed.

Dad had three locks on his front door. He even locked the door after us once we were in. The estate was pretty rough.

I went into the main room and stared out of the window. This was the view that Dad had every day. A stretch of patchy tarmac with a row of bins and a car without wheels that had been vandalised. There was a decaying concrete block of flats opposite whose doors and windows had been painted in optimistically bright colours: orange and turquoise, which somehow made the damp-stained buildings look even more bleak.

It seemed so crazy that once he'd had a house and a garden in a nice street and now all he had was this. Surely he couldn't prefer it to living with me and Mum?

'You can't *like* living here,' I blurted out.

Dad shrugged. 'It's all I can afford. Anyway, it's central and I've got a lock-up down below for the bike.'

I wanted to shout at him. To tell him to get back to his senses. It wasn't too late. They weren't divorced yet. But I just said, 'It all seems so crazy.'

'It's not really living here that's the problem.'

'What d'you mean?'

'You get lonely living alone. It would be the same anywhere.'

'Well, exactly. That's what I've been trying to say.'

'Well. I'll have to do something about it. Won't I?'

'Yes.'

'I might surprise you one of these days.' Dad gave a secret smile and rubbed his hands together.

I wasn't having any of that. 'Come on, you can't start a topic like that then simply drop it.'

'Nah, don't pester. You'll know all about it, sooner or later.'

Sooner or later! If Mum and Dad were thinking about getting back together I should be the *first* to know. I pressed harder. But Dad wouldn't be pressurised. He just insisted that it was too early to say anything. But he was working on it.

'Trust me,' he said, giving me a hug. 'Come on, let's forget that I ever said anything.' He took the carriers of food into the kitchen to sort out the meal.

I went on a little tour of investigation round the flat. The tiny bedroom that had been planned for me, now housed his darkroom. I peeped inside. The smell of the chemicals brought on a great wave of nostalgia. I remembered how Dad and I used to develop films together in the old days. He'd let me take the tongs and dip the prints into the trays of developer. I loved the way a shadowy face would form, appearing as if by magic through the liquid, getting more and more contrast until, sharp and glossy, the print was ready to hang up to dry. Dad seemed to have lost interest in photography recently. But today he had some black and white prints hanging on their little pegs.

'Hey, you're doing your own developing again,' I called to him, trying to make them out in the gloom. There was one of me with Mum and Dad on a holiday we'd had long long ago. Someone must've taken it for us. I looked about six, standing in front, grinning with a front tooth missing. Mum and Dad were behind. Dad had his arm round Mum. They looked really happy.

Dad came to the door and looked in.

'It was good, that holiday, wasn't it?' I prompted.

'Yeah,' he said. 'Yeah, it was.' Then he abruptly changed the subject. 'How about lunch then? Hungry? I'm famished.'

'OK,' I said, following him into the kitchen. 'So what have you got?'

'Health food,' he said. 'I'm on a diet.'

'You? On a diet?'

With a flourish he emptied out the carriers on to the kitchen table. There was a plastic bag of pre-washed salad, a jar of beetroot, a bunch of celery, a bag of carrots and some apples.

'*Health* food! You're turning into a rabbit.'

We spent the next half hour scraping and chopping until we'd made a huge mixed salad. Dad poured some oil and vinegar dressing over it. We ate it with hot nut bread. It was yummy.

'How are you and your Mum managing?' asked Dad as we finished our meal. 'For money I mean?'

It was good to hear he cared. 'We're OK. Of

course the car's on its last legs.'

'I'll see what I can do. Your mum still out a lot?'

'Only at her rehearsals. She seems to really enjoy it. I guess it gets her out to meet people.'

'What, like other blokes?' he asked.

I paused. From what Mum had said, it sounded as if most of the other actors were women, but I wasn't going to tell him that. A little competition never did any harm.

'I haven't actually met any of the other actors yet,' I said. 'But they sound like Mum's kind of people. Into books and stuff, you know.'

'Uh-huh. So, what have you been up to then?' asked Dad as he put the kettle on to make coffee.

'Oh, nothing much. Getting to know the neighbours.'

'Anyone your age?'

'Not really.'

'Your mum said there's a boy on the third floor.'

(They *had* been communicating, then.) 'Oh, that's *Cedric*.'

'What's wrong with him?'

'Nothing. He's not my type, that's all. I've set him up with Clare as a matter of fact.'

'Is he Clare's type?'

'Umm, I reckon with a bit of fine tuning, he could be.'

'Fine tuning?'

'I'm working on it.'

He gave me a sideways look. 'What about you? Don't you need a boyfriend?'

'Not till I find complete *perfection*. No.'

'That's my girl.'

We finished the afternoon with a walk in Dad's local park. I gave him a crash course in aerobic-walking. We were halfway round our second circuit and he was steaming on ahead when I noticed he was turning red in the face.

'You shouldn't overdo it, you know,' I warned.

'Want to get in shape for the pool,' he gasped.

'Pool? What pool?'

'Ah,' he said, slowing up a little. 'I've been meaning to tell you. I'm thinking of taking a bit of a break.' (Dad had been talking of taking me away with him next holidays. Somewhere like Paris or Amsterdam. I'd been looking forward to it.)

'When?'

'Ten days' time.'

'But that's not the holidays. It's still term-time.'

'I know. That's why it's a really good deal. The two

of us could go away another time, maybe.'

I tried not to look disappointed. 'Where are you going?'

'Spain.'

'What, all on your own?'

'Look, Jessica. I need a change.' (He never called me Jessica, unless he was cross.)

'I see. Well, I guess you'll get a tan,' I said, trying to sound positive.

'Mmm, and get rid of some of this,' he said, patting his belly.

'That's if you lay off the beer.'

'You know, I might just do that.'

'Good.'

I left him outside his block of flats with strict instructions to use stairs in future instead of taking the lift.

I made my way back to Rosemount with mixed feelings. Of course I was disappointed about not going with him. But maybe, just maybe, I was making headway. Joined the gym. Eating *health* food. And thinking of giving up beer. It wasn't a bad start.

On the train on the way back I got a text message from Clare.

where are you?
wobble

I texted her back.

happy cruising!
love j

I arrived at my station, wondering if Cedric had made it. I didn't have to wonder for long. Another text followed fast, this time from Cedric

so where are you?

I texted him back:

so sorry
i forgot i had to meet dad!

I walked from the tube station to Rosemount, happy in the knowledge that Clare and Cedric were now, quite definitely, an item.

I got back to Rosemount to find Mum ironing in the kitchen. She had a huge mass of material, looked like curtains.

'Have a nice lunch?'

'Yes, as a matter of fact. At his place.'

'Really? What did you eat?'

'Salad! He made it.'

'*Salad?*'

'Mmm. At last, he's starting to take care of himself. He's going on holiday too. Did you know he was going to Spain?'

'Oh, so he's told you?'

'You *did* know?'

'Well, he did mention it.'

'Why didn't you say anything?'

'I was going to.' She paused from her ironing. 'How much did he tell you?'

'Only that he was going to Marbella for a week.'

She refilled the iron with water. 'I thought you'd be upset he wasn't taking you.'

'I am. Why couldn't he wait for the summer holidays?'

'I think he needs some time on his own. To think things over.'

She was being very supportive of him all of a sudden. 'What sort of things?'

'Oh, just things,' she said, and then she dragged the material off the ironing board. 'Come on, can you help me with this?'

'What on earth is it?'

'My costume. I'm trying to alter it.'

'Looks like a giant tea-cosy,' I commented.

'If I get into it, could you see if you could pin it in at the back?'

I spent the next half hour struggling with the costume and trying not to pin Mum with it. It was a heavy damask material dotted with big fat false gems. It had been made for someone twice her size.

'There you go,' I said as I put the last pin in.

We both stared at her reflection in the mirror. 'It'll look better with the wig,' she said.

'And maybe without your glasses?'

'Hmm.'

'To think things over.' *Things?* I thought as I went to my room. Mum was being very mysterious. Both of them were. They'd been talking on the phone. Dad had to go away to '*think things over*'. Like them getting back together? Mum had been looking a lot happier recently. I was getting more and more certain that my plan was working.

Later, while I was sorting through my wardrobe for something to wear to Marie's party, Clare rang. 'What happened to you?' she asked.

'Thought you needed some time alone together.'

'You are the most evil, scheming witch on this earth,' she exclaimed.

I took this as a compliment. 'How did it go?'

'It was so-oo, so-oo brilliant!'

'Tell me everything.'

She then bent my ear for a good half hour on how funny Cedric had been and how they'd talked non-stop . . . She ended with, 'And on the way back I saw this dress. It's perfect.'

'Perfect for what?'

'For the Cranshaw Ball, of course.'

'Has he asked you?'

'No, not yet. But he kind of hinted at it.'

'How?'

'We were talking about our GCSE French trip – and I told him when it was and then he said good 'cos it didn't clash.'

I lay in bed that night totting up my successes. Clare and Cedric were well on the way. Cedric was defi-nitely getting interested. And Clare was shaping up nicely too. And then there was Mum and Dad. Little echoes of our conversation ran through my head: *'You get lonely living alone . . . I'll have to do something about it . . . Too early to say . . .'*

My mind drifted on to Jane and Henry. Sigh. I wasn't getting far on that one. The purple envelope was in my drawer, *taunting me*. They were out there somewhere. People didn't just dematerialise. I vowed I'd get them together, if it was the last thing I did.

chapter eleven

On Monday, at school, I made a pact with myself that I was going to bring my averages up to prove to Mum and Dad that I was truly making an effort. Particularly in English. I would show Mr Williams that he had cruelly misjudged me. Just because he could write a measly rubbish play for his amateur dramatics, didn't mean he knew *everything*. So when he asked for a volunteer to read out their *Romeo and Juliet* essay, I was the first to put up my hand.

We were meant to be commenting on the modern screen version starring Claire Danes and Leonardo Di Caprio, and comparing it with the original play. I'd actually spent rather more time looking at the video of the film than reading Shakespeare's version (well, that didn't have Leonardo in it). But I was pretty pleased with my essay all the same.

'Good, Jessica,' said Mr Williams, spotting my

hand. 'It's nice to see you being so enthusiastic.'

I got up and cleared my throat. 'The original play gives us a picture of life in Shakespeare's time. Women like Juliet had no rights. It is making a *social comment*,' I said, glancing meaningfully at Mr Williams (you see, I had learned a lesson from my *Pygmalion* essay). He nodded encouragingly. 'The trouble with the screen version is that it's not true to life. What really would have happened would have been more like this:

'Act Four. Scene Six. Somewhere on the road to Mantua. Leonardo Di Caprio—'

Mr Williams interrupted. 'By which, Jessica, I assume you mean Romeo . . .'

' . . . Romeo,' I corrected myself, 'is on his motor-bike. His mobile is ringing.

'Leonardo, errm, I mean Romeo (answering it): "Fair Juliet, how fare ye?"

'Juliet (voice-over all echoey): "Don't ask! I'm in this fearful spooky tomb. Make haste my love, speed back to my side and save me."

'*Romeo* (swerving his bike round – aerial shot): "T'will be with you in a jiffy—"'

'Jessica . . . ' Mr Williams interrupted just as I was getting to the good bit. I put my essay down and turned to him with a patient expression.

'You were asked, Jessica, to compare and contrast the film and the play, not rewrite it. Don't you ever read the question?'

'But Mr Williams. Juliet wasn't stupid. If it was meant to be modern day, she'd never have dreamt of going down into that tomb without her mobile.'

Several people in the class agreed with me at that point. And general mayhem broke out as the swots in the front row supported Mr Williams while the cool crowd, who sat at the back, leaped to my defence. When Mr Williams had regained order, he said, 'Sit down please, Jessica.'

I sat down and listened, rebelling inwardly, while he droned on and on about text and context and something he called 'truth to the original'. As he moved on round the class out of my sightlines I reached for my mobile under the desk and texted Clare.

mr w is such a ploncker!
why doesn't he get a life?

As luck would have it Mr Williams happened to be passing Clare at that moment. He swooped on her mobile and put it in his pocket, saying that 'if he was in a good mood' she could have it back at the end of the day.

It was towards the end of the period, when we were working in groups deciphering a sonnet, that Mr Williams moved to the front of the class.

'That'll be all for today. I hope you'll *all* remember in future the school rule – all mobiles switched off while on the premises, please. And just for the record, Jessica, there is no "c" in plonker.'

I walked down to lunch fuming, Mr W's comment rankling in my mind. How can he be so-oo arrogant. *'Just for the record, Jessica, there is no "c" in plonker'* . . . Huh! Now he was going to be down on me more then ever. Loads of the class could see I had a point. It was so unfair.

Clare was already in the lunch queue. I took a tray and slid in beside her.

'So sorry he nabbed your mobile.'

'It's not your fault. I reckon he's got an in-built mobile sensor. Why's he so down on you, anyway?'

'I dunno.'

Clare refused all the hot meals and went for a salad. She wouldn't even put dressing on it. She was

160

really taking this diet thing seriously. I watched her cutting her lettuce into shreds and putting little *mouse* mouthfuls on her fork.

'You can eat as much *salad* as you like,' I commented.

'Thanks,' she said. '*You* can eat as much chocolate as you like.'

She needn't be like that. I had actually cut out a lot of things in order to be supportive. I'd selected a single burger with salad and no fries. And I hadn't had a Mars bar for at least two days. You'd have thought so much self-discipline on my part would have made a difference, but I suppose she'd only been on her diet for a week. I hoped it would start working soon. I didn't know how much longer I could hold out.

Christine was at a neighbouring table with her habitual semicircle of fawning admirers. I raised an eyebrow at Clare and she made a face back. We sat with our backs to them, but as we ate we couldn't help catching snatches of their conversation.

'Matt's going to hire a limo to take us to the ball. There's this company that does white Mercedes . . . He's got his own dinner jacket . . .'

Clare put down her fork with a sigh and pushed her plate away.

'Look, I know Cedric really likes you,' I whispered comfortingly. 'He just hasn't got round to asking.'

'But time's running out,' said Clare.

Christine got up to go and came in our direction. There was only a tiny little gap between two tables and she ostentatiously slid her incredibly lean bottom between them and wafted off.

Clare watched her with ill-disguised envy. 'I bet that dress will be gone by the time he invites me,' she said.

'Maybe we should try something more drastic.'

'Like what?'

'I reckon he needs some competition. When you're together, what if someone, like some other boy, kept texting you?'

'Not a bad idea. But who?'

'It doesn't have to be a real boy, dumbo.'

'Oh, I get what you mean.'

Clare insisted I went with her after school to check the dress out. It was in Top Knotch, the young designer department of Braithwaites. A place we never usually shopped in because it was far too expensive.

Clare hauled the dress out from the rack and held

it up to her. 'What do you think?'

It was strapless and in pale silver shimmery satin, the kind of dress that's guaranteed to make you look twice your normal size. I checked the tag. 'Have you seen the price!' I said.

'Can't you see this is really important?'

'Anyway,' I continued, running through the rack. 'It's the only one they've got and it's a size ten.'

Clare gave me a resentful look. 'By the time of the ball, I'll *be* a size ten,' she said with determination. I watched in silence as she asked the assistant to put it aside for her. The assistant said she could only keep it for a limited time.

The dress meant that Clare really put the pressure on. The invitation to the ball, or rather lack of it, literally became her only topic of conversation. I needed to put the pressure on. But in order to test out the texting tactic, I had to get Clare and Cedric together. No chance occurred until Friday when I got off early from school, and bumped into Cedric on the stairs.

'What you doing later?' he asked.

I thought fast. 'Going over to Clare's place.'

'All right if I come with you?'

'Sure.' (There, you see! Easy!)

'Promised I'd fix her bike,' he said. (Isn't that sweet?)

'OK, see you 'bout four and we can go together.'

Cedric turned up at my door at the dot of four wearing immaculate new black jeans – not the sort of thing you'd normally mend a bike in, but he was carrying a bag of tools.

We arrived at Clare's place to find that she had already taken her bike out of the garden shed in readiness. It was pretty obvious that it was an excuse to get Cedric over. Anyone could see it hadn't been ridden for years. It was covered in rust.

I watched from the kitchen window as Cedric took it apart. It had started to drizzle, but Clare's mum, who's paranoid about her house, insisted that the job was done outside. Clare was eagerly helping, running back and forth with bowls of water and kitchen towel. Cedric soon had loads of tiny components laid out on their terrace. His new jeans were getting covered in oil and rust. The job was going to take ages. (The things people do for love!)

While they were busy with the bike I popped upstairs to the bathroom and took the opportunity to send Clare a message. I scrolled down through the Cs in my phone book. Carol, Cedric, Clare . . . Nothing too extreme for a first message. I tapped in a fairly neutral but obviously boyish message and added a frieze of XXXXs. That should do it.

I peered through the window and saw Clare checking her mobile. Cedric was looking over her shoulder. Nice one! Clare clicked her mobile shut and I could see that a certain amount of teasing was going on below as to who the message might be from. Clare was making a big thing about not telling. Cedric was obviously intrigued.

I decided to leave them to it and made the excuse that I had to get back to Rosemount to help Mum learn her lines. On the way back in the bus I sent Clare a couple more rather keener messages.

I got back to Rosemount to find Roz in the lobby battling to fold up her pram. She was trying to get it into the lift complete with baby and shopping. The baby was balanced on one shoulder and as usual it was howling.

'Thanks,' she shouted as I took over the job of pram-folding. 'Can't leave it in the hall. The last one got stolen.'

I went up to her floor with her and helped her into her flat. 'Want a cup of tea?' she asked, as she slammed around with bottles and formula.

I found the kettle upturned in the sink and filled it. While she made up the baby's bottle I managed to find tea bags and some sugar. The milk in the fridge had congealed to a kind of yogurt so we had to settle for black.

At last the baby was sucking at his bottle and we got some peace. Roz then gave me a crash course on how not to ruin your life. As she finished she was near to tears.

'But that's awful,' I said. 'Don't you ever get out in the evening?' Before I knew it, I found I'd volunteered to baby-sit.

'Oh, would you?' said Roz, her tears magically drying.

'Of course, I've got loads of homework to do. I could easily bring it down here.'

'You couldn't manage tonight, could you?' she pleaded. 'I've been invited to this gig by the guys downstairs.'

'Which guys?'

'Barry and Jeremy. They live at number three.' Number three was Jekyll and Hyde's apartment – so there *were* two of them. I wondered which one Roz was after.

I agreed to be back at 8 p.m. The baby-sitting had provided a handy excuse for me too. Cedric had invited Clare and me over to his place later. Now I had a water-tight excuse for leaving them alone.

I was coming out of Roz's flat when I bumped into Cedric on the stairs.

'So did you get the bike mended?'

'Yeah. Kind of. Clare was meant to be helping. But she didn't do much, she kept getting these text messages.' He sounded most put out. (I think I could be forgiven for a little glow of triumph at this point.)

'Any more letters from you-know-who?' he asked.

'Who?'

'That anonymous person.'

'Oh him. No.'

'You still on for tonight?'

'Oh no, can't. I've promised to baby-sit for the girl in number six. But Clare is.'

'Oh right, sure,' said Cedric.

chapter twelve

That night I had my revised *Romeo and Juliet* essay to write, which would help pass the time. At around seven-thirty Mum got back, loaded with supermarket carriers – she'd done the weekly shop. I helped her unpack and stock the fridge.

'You couldn't spare the time to hear my lines, could you?'

'Can't, sorry. I've said I'd baby-sit for the girl in number six.'

'Oh, that's nice of you.'

'Just so long as she briefs me properly. I've no idea about babies.'

'Good practice.'

'Practice for what? I'm not thinking of having babies till I'm at least thirty.'

'But you might have a brother or sister some day.'

I stared at Mum.

'Surely not!'

She laughed. 'No need to look at me like that. I'm not totally over the hill, you know.'

Jeez! I thought. And then I thought, why not? If Mum and Dad did get back together there was no reason why they shouldn't have another child. It might be just what they needed.

I left Mum muttering over her lines and took my books downstairs to Roz's flat. She'd accomplished an amazing transformation. Washed her hair, got clean jeans on and even a half-way decent jacket. The baby was quiet for once. She beckoned to me and we crept to the door of the room he was sleeping in. There was a low light on inside. I could just see his little face and tight fist sticking out from under the quilt.

'He should sleep till midnight,' whispered Roz. 'But if he wakes up I've got a bottle ready. Just give him that. He may need changing. The nappies are right here. And the baby wipes and baby lotion. And you'll need to check that he doesn't get too hot. If he does, he'll be thirsty and you can give him juice which hardly needs warming . . . '

I was starting to wish I'd taken notes. 'Fine,' I said, trying to sound more confident than I felt.

'I'll be back by eleven thirty,' she whispered.

'Don't worry about a thing. Have a good time.' I closed the door as quietly as I could behind her.

Having peeped in one more time on the baby and established that he was sleeping peacefully, I cleared a space on the coffee table and got out my books. Taking the *Romeo and Juliet* essay out of my file, I took a deep breath and started writing: *The tragedy all hinged on the letter* . . . (I felt a pang of guilt at that).

I put down my pen. If the letter from Friar Lawrence had got to Romeo in time, he would have known that Juliet was only faking death. Then there would have been this brilliant moment when Di Caprio (errm, I mean Romeo) would have lifted Juliet up and carried her out of the tomb. Everyone would have thought it was some sort of miracle and so they would probably have let them get married after all . . . Which would've been a so-oo much better ending . . .

Which got me thinking. If Henry's letter had got to Jane, their romance would have ended happily too. I could imagine them now, having dinner together, soft lighting from candles on the table, a bunch of long red roses (Henry's gift) in a tall vase. Each plate laid out with artfully arranged food, king prawns maybe, with those little chef's hats on their tails. Soft background music. But no. Thanks to me they were each in their separate flats, each microwaving their lone TV dinner . . .

I simply couldn't go on with my essay until I'd done something about it. I took the purple envelope out of my backpack and stared at it. That's when it occurred to me that perhaps I *did* know where Henry was. I had his address on my clipboard, the one that I'd got from the blokes in the pub. That's if he was the right Henry – there must be thousands of Henrys around. Yet it all fitted. Where he lived – Forest Vale – and the card and the pen and everything. With resolution I took out a clean sheet of file paper and wrote:

Dear Henry,
You don't know me. And this may sound very odd but I really have to speak to you in person. Please would you meet me at 11 a.m. next Saturday 12th May at Muggins Café in the mall.
Yours,
A friend

I folded the letter carefully, slid it into an envelope and wrote 'To Henry' followed by the address. Next

Saturday I'd get the bus back to Forest Vale and check him out.

That's when I suddenly became aware that there was a sound coming from the baby's room. A slight shuddering sobbing noise. Well, he'd probably go back to sleep if I didn't do anything. I continued my essay.

The sobbing grew louder. I gave up writing and went into his room. The baby didn't take kindly to a stranger appearing. He took one look at me and let rip. I had no idea something so small could make so much noise. I tried making comforting noises like I had to Bag when he was a kitten. Then I picked him up. A baby is much heavier than a cat and this one was revoltingly damp. The bed was really wet too. Comforting cat noises didn't go down at all well. He was getting redder and redder in the face. He made me think of those dolls which schools lend teenagers with the aim of putting them off babies. I'm telling you now, they are nowhere near as good as the real thing. This baby could keep a girl on contraception till she was way past child-bearing age.

I tried desperately to remember Roz's instructions. Milk, that was the thing. I lugged the baby into the kitchen. The bottle of formula stood ready in a bottle warmer. I kept my head, despite the decibels, testing the milk for temperature.

At last, I had baby on lap, bottle in mouth. The baby sucked, eyeing me warily round the bottle. You could tell from the way he looked at me that he had no confidence in my ability. It took him about fifteen minutes to get halfway through the milk and then he kept falling asleep. So I had to jiggle him to wake him up.

I took the opportunity of relative peace to text Clare. Jogging the baby with one arm, I scrolled down through the Cs in my phone-book, and was just sending what I flattered myself was an artfully sexy text message when . . . Ooops! a load of slimy sick slid down my jumper. The baby had clearly indicated he didn't want any more milk.

It didn't seem right simply to dump him in bed in his soggy state, so I gritted my teeth. I won't go into the nappy changing bit. I'll only say that I was the one that came off worse. Somehow I got him back in a dry nappy, dry clothes and a dry bed. He lay there staring at me, whimpering. So I picked up a pink nylon bunny and threatened him with it. Miraculously, this was greeted by a toothless grin. I shook the bunny again. Another grin. It's so easy when you know how.

I left him cooing and gurgling in possession of the bunny and crept out. He'd got what he wanted. The fact that I was utterly demoralised, wet through and covered in sick didn't seem to bother him one bit. Back in the kitchen I wearily loaded the wet bedding into the washer-dryer. Then I stripped off and added my T-shirt and jeans as well, making do with the hideous floral robe of Roz's that I found on a hook in the bathroom. I turned the washer on.

My phone was ringing. It was Clare.

'Hi. Where are you?'

'On the way back home.' She sounded depressed.

'What? Why? Did you get my message?'

'What message?'

'The one I just sent you.'

'No . . . I didn't get any message.'

'That's funny. I wonder what happened to it. Has he asked you yet?'

'No.'

'What went wrong?'

'I don't know.'

'*Men.*'

'Hmm.'

'Well, cheer up. There's still time.' Odd, I thought,

as I went back into the living room and got back to my homework.

It was twenty minutes later that the poltergeists struck. I sat rooted to my seat as I heard things being flung around the kitchen. My hair was practically standing on end. I immediately thought of *the baby*. He was blotchy, red-faced, decidedly evil-looking. I had this sudden flashback: 'Roz. My name's Roz.' What could Roz be short for but *Rosemary*.

I couldn't move from the chair for fear. I groped for my mobile. There was nothing else for it. I rang Cedric's number. To my undying gratitude he answered right away.

'Jessica? You sound weird. What's up?'

'Listen. I can't move. You've got to come and save me.'

'Where are you?'

'Upstairs at number six. You know, *baby*-sitting. Please come now.'

'I'll be right up.'

Within seconds he was ringing on the doorbell. I steeled myself and, without looking to right or left, I flung myself at the door.

'I'm so glad to see you,' I gasped, clinging to him.

'Hey, cool it.' He disentangled himself. 'What's the trouble?'

'They're in the kitchen,' I whispered.

'Who?'

'Poltergeists. They're flinging things about. Listen!' There was a low rumbling sound and more sounds of shattering crockery. We both stared at the knob of the kitchen door.

'OK, right. Stand back,' said Cedric, steeling himself.

He flung the door open. Inside, the washing machine was doing a lumbering walk across the floor. Cedric strode in and pulled the plug from the wall. There was a sudden silence.

'Uneven load,' he said. 'Jeesus, Jessica, you've got an overactive imagination.'

'No I haven't.'

'What made you think of poltergeists?'

There was a wail from the baby's room. 'That's Rosemary's baby,' I said weakly.

Cedric cracked up. I didn't think it was so funny.

'What *have* you got on?' he asked.

I suddenly became aware that the odds had changed. He was being strong and forceful while I was being a wimp. What's more I was standing there wearing Roz's hideous floral robe.

Cedric + being forceful > Jessica + being wimpy

Ce + bf > J + bw

Or to simplify:

Ce > J *Surely not!*

There was a pause.

'Look,' he said. 'I got your message.' He took a step closer to me.

'What message?' I said, backing away a step.

'The one you texted me.'

'I texted you?' I stared at him as the terrible truth dawned on me. I could see myself scrolling through my phone-book down to 'Clare'. Through 'Carol, Cedric . . . ' Quite obviously, with all the distractions from the baby, I hadn't got to Clare – and nor had my artfully sexy message. Oops!

'I was really, you know – knocked out by it,' he said. He took another step towards me. I took another step back. O-m-G. What should I do now? I could hardly tell him the message was meant for Clare or I'd give the game away. All I could think of was to get rid of him as quickly as possible. With helpful timing the baby started crying again.

'Look, you'd better go,' I said. 'He doesn't like strangers.' I virtually bundled Cedric out of the door and closed it behind him. I stood there leaning against it, my mind racing.

This had put me totally off my stride.

chapter thirteen

The following Monday I posted my letter to Henry on the way to school and continued with a lighter heart. At least I was doing *something*.

The bus arrived. Clare had saved a seat for me as usual. I climbed in beside her.

'So what am I doing wrong?' she demanded.

'Nothing!' I replied, feeling really guilty. I had a horrible flashback of my message. Oh, why had it gone to *Cedric*, of all people?

'But I must be. I was being really interested in his music and his bike and everything but he simply didn't react.'

'Maybe you seemed too keen.'

'You think so?'

'You have to kind of encourage males without seeming too desperate.'

'You think I'm acting like desperate?'

'No, not desperate exactly, but you know males. You have to kind of get them interested by being interested but not *too* interested.'

'And you think that I'm being *too* interested?'

'Exactly. Look, from now on, cool it. Pretend he doesn't exist.'

'I'll try.'

Once inside school, I met Mr Williams in the corridor. He asked me if I'd finished my revised *Romeo and Juliet* essay. When I said 'almost' he practically self-combusted. He said that if I didn't have it in by lunchtime, which meant twelve-thirty on-the-dot, he would have to give me a failure grade for it which would bring my coursework average down even further.

'But Mr Williams. I'll never get it done by lunchtime.'

'That, Jessica, is your problem,' he said, and made off down the corridor.

Luckily the next class was double art. Now art *really is* my best subject. I was nicely ahead with my coursework. With any luck I could persuade Ms Mills to let me have an hour or so in the library to finish the essay.

I took my work out of my portfolio. They were studies for a still life of three oranges and a bowl of goldfish. I placed my sketches in a prominent position for inspection. I expected praise from Ms Mills. I sat with a modestly non-commital expression waiting for it while she went through my portfolio. She looked up with a frown. A *frown*!?

'Yes, a good start as usual, Jessica. But I must say you've still a lot more work to put in. Especially on this final study . . . '

(More work? That final colour study was *brilliant*. I was thinking of entering it for the Turner Prize, as a matter of fact.)

' . . . for a still life, it's very angular.'

'But that's the point, Ms Mills. It's my tribute to Futurism.' (Couldn't she *see*?)

'Sometimes, Jessica, I think you're trying to run before you can walk. *Square* oranges?'

Run? Hadn't she noticed the twentieth century? A whole hundred years has taken place since *anyone* had painted what she would call a *good* still life (something circa 1910 – definitely *before* Cezanne).

I was instructed to redo the final study. 'Remember cold-warm-cold, dear. Oranges are *round*, Jessica. In case you hadn't noticed.'

'But Ms Mills, I was hoping you might let me have some time off to work in the library. I'm a bit behind on an English ess—'

'Out of the question, Jessica. Not when you've got so much to catch up on.'

I sat for the next hour obediently doing totally unoriginal perfectly rounded oranges in pastel and watching the minutes tick by on the art-room clock. Each one of them bringing me nearer and nearer to being a GCSE English failure. I'd never be a writer now. And it was all Mr Williams's fault. Twelve-thirty came and went. The bell rang for lunch, irrevocably sealing my fate.

I made my way miserably down to the canteen. Clare was there already.

'What's up?'

'Everything,' I moaned.

'Like what?'

I explained about my *Romeo and Juliet* essay and my brilliant tribute to Futurism.

'You can imagine what it's doing for my course-work averages. It's not fair, Mr Williams is being so anal. And Ms Mills is really down on me.'

'You know why, don't you?'

'No?'

'It's obvious. Neither of them is married, or has a partner as far as we know. It's clearly sexual frustration, and they're taking it out on us.'

'You think?'

'Definitely.'

I paused in the middle of a forkful of shepherd's pie. They were both really into art.

Ms Mills + art – poodle hairdo + great smile. And Mr Williams + art – worn cords + nice hair. Or to put it more scientifically:

$$MsM + a - ph + gs = MrW + a - wc + nh$$

Or maybe:

$$\frac{MsM - ph + gs = MrW - wc + nh}{a} \quad \textit{Nice Match!}$$

'I've just had an idea,' I said. 'Don't you think that they would be just perfect for each other?'

'What, Ms Mills and Mr Williams?' Clare chewed on a radish thoughtfully. 'Umm, well . . . I dunno, maybe.'

'But they are.'

'In which case, why haven't they got together?'

I shrugged. 'Perhaps they need help.'

'What sort of help?'

'Like something to throw them together.'

'Like what? Locking them up together in the supplies store?'

'Maybe something a bit more subtle.' I wracked my brain. It needed to be something outside school. Some accidental meeting . . . Then it occurred to me. 'Does your sister still get those free theatre tickets?' Clare's sister was a nurse. Her hospital was always getting hand-outs of free tickets for plays that nobody wanted to see.

'Mmm. In fact, she's got some she can't use this Saturday, I think.'

'Could you bring them in tomorrow?'

'What are you up to?'

'Just a little idea of mine.'

'You'll *never* get those two together.'

'Wanna bet?'

Next day I offered to clean the art-room sink after double art. Ms Mills was pottering around as usual collecting up brushes and putting paper away, so we had the room to ourselves. I said, ever so casually, 'Ms Mills, do you like the theatre?'

'Why do you ask, Jessica?'

'It's just that I've been given this free ticket for the preview of the Brecht play at the Almeida and I can't go. It seems such a waste not to use it. I was looking for someone who's, you know, a bit cultural, to give it to.'

'Well, how thoughtful of you, Jessica.' Ms Mills sounded flattered. 'When's it for?'

'This Saturday.'

'Saturday. Yes. I'd like it very much. If you're sure there's no one else you want to give it to.'

I handed it over to her. It was so easy. Now for Mr Williams.

I came across him at breaktime putting up the poster for his play on the Arts Activities noticeboard.

I coughed politely to attract his attention. He turned and nearly jumped out of his skin at seeing me standing there.

'Oh, Jessica! What can I do for you?' He looked really hot and uncomfortable for some reason. Probably regretting how terribly unfair he had been about my *Romeo and Juliet* essay.

'I just wondered, Mr Williams, seeing as you're so interested in the theatre, whether you might like this ticket I can't use. It's for the Brecht play at the Almeida.' I held it out for him to see.

Mr Williams got his glasses out of his top pocket. 'Oh . . . ooh. How nice of you, Jessica. Yes, I was thinking of going to it, as a matter of fact. Are you sure you can't use the ticket? Or change it for another night maybe? I wouldn't like you to miss the opportunity to experience Brecht live.'

'It's a complimentary, Mr Williams. And I can't make Saturday.'

'Then I accept with pleasure. Most thoughtful of you.' He put the ticket in his pocket.

I positively floated down the corridor to my locker, envisaging Saturday night and *love blossoming* in the centre stalls. I texted Clare right away.

nice match!
ms m and mr w sat night
row g seats no. 25 and 26 ♥

I lay in bed that night happily visualising Mr Williams and Ms Mills sitting side by side in the Almeida. Sharing a box of chocolates maybe. Having a drink together in the bar in the interval, laughing in a slightly embarrassed way about the coincidence that had brought them together. Later, he'd offer to drive her home, and then maybe she'd invite him in for coffee . . .

chapter fourteen

So much for Mr Williams and Ms Mills. Now for Jane and Henry. That Saturday was the day I was due to go to Forest Vale. Henry would have received my letter by now. He *had* to be there and he *had* to be the right Henry.

I washed my hair and used tons of conditioner and blow-dried it so that it was really shiny. I'd even washed my favourite jeans the night before and tumble dried them so that they shrank to an optimum fit. Not that it mattered, of course, what I looked like – I was only finding Henry for Jane.

The bus that morning seemed to take for ever, stopping at umpteen random stops which I hadn't remembered from the previous journey. I arrived early at the café all the same. I peered through the steamy windows. There was no one who looked as if they could possibly be Henry. Venturing inside, I found the café's customers consisted of two blue-rinse ladies who were taking a break from shopping and an old man with a mangy dog and a pile of newspapers who looked as if he lived in the place. I bought myself a coffee and chose a table near a window away from the others and waited.

Each time the door opened with a jangle of the bell, I nearly jumped out of my skin. But the only people who turned up were a jogger who wanted a bottle of mineral water and a woman who came in collecting for charity.

I kept glancing at my watch – the minute hand seemed to be on a go-slow. Eleven o'clock came and went. By eleven forty-five I was starting to give up hope. I rubbed a place clear in the steamy window. And at that moment, this fit-looking guy appeared inside the circle of steam like the hero of an old movie. *He was coming straight for the café.*

He opened the door and looked around. My jaw dropped. This boy was *gorgeous*. Divine bright blue eyes met mine. In spite of myself my mind did a lightning calculation:

Did his sexy blue eyes, fit body, nice smile lines, high cheekbones, perfectly faded jeans, cool leather jacket, latest trainers, *equal* my nice, shiny, blow-dried hair, long legs and straight teeth (thanks to two years of an agonising fixed brace), errm, nice-fitting jeans, not bad T-shirt, decent nails (I'd stopped biting them), errm (I tried to think of more positives but I was really scraping the barrel now).

$$H + (sbe + fb + nsl + hcb + pfj + clj + lt) = J + (nsbdh + ll + st + nfj + nbTs + dn)$$ *Match Pl-ease?*

Because frankly, I wouldn't substitute a single thing about him.

But could this be Henry? He was slightly shy-looking. A little young perhaps to suggest *marriage*. But then some people married really young, didn't they? Lucky Jane. I hoped she appreciated him. I'd hardly be human if I hadn't felt just a flicker of envy. No, more than a flicker – the green serpent shifted and stretched and recoiled itself inside me. I reassessed my image of Jane. Suddenly she had thinner lips, and there was a cold calculating look in her eyes. She certainly didn't deserve him. What Henry needed was someone understanding. Somebody more like *me*.

I had decided most definitely.

Henry > Jane

I held my breath. He was obviously looking for someone. The blue-rinse ladies and the elderly man with the dog were unlikely candidates. Which only left me.

He caught my eye again and half-smiled and nodded. I smiled back, waiting for him to say something. But he seemed to be waiting for me to. I couldn't think of how to start. This was just so embarrassing.

He turned away and went to the counter and bought a Coke. Drink in hand he took a circuit of the room that passed my table. Our eyes met again. He took a sip out of his Coke bottle and gazed around the café as if someone might magically materialise out of thin air. Then he turned and *started to make for the door*.

I couldn't simply give up like this. 'Wait!' I said.

He turned back to face me. 'Yes?'

'Are you Henry?' I blurted out.

'Are you "*A friend*"?' he asked.

I nodded, blushing to the roots of my hair. This must seem like the most obvious pick-up in the history of the universe. Having come so far I couldn't give up now. I *had* to do it. I reached in my pocket and passed him the envelope.

He raised his eyebrows and pulled out a chair. 'May I?'

I nodded and he sat down at my table. With a look of concentration he drew out the card. (Oh, why did it have to be such a naff card?) I cringed as he read the message on the front: '*To someone special*'.

One look at his face told me instantly. 'Oh my God. It's not from you, is it?'

He shook his head.

I was getting up from my seat. 'This is just so embarrassing. Forget it even happened, OK? You . . . me . . . we were never here. Right?'

'But . . . ' he started.

'No, really. I've made a stupid mistake.' All I wanted was to get out of the café as fast as I could. If only the stained linoleum floor would swallow me up. If only I could put my life on rewind and do a retake.

I could hear my bus revving up at the stop, preparing to leave. 'That's my bus,' I said, groping for my backpack.

He reached the door before me. As I pushed it open our hands met. Well, maybe only the tips of our fingers. But the touch went through me like electricity. He was smiling in a way that made me smile back. I suddenly realised I was so, so glad he wasn't the right Henry.

'It's too late. You won't catch that bus now,' he

said. He was right. It was already picking up speed, accelerating away from the stop. 'Why don't you let me buy you a coffee and tell me what this is all about?'

I sat down in my seat again. 'You promise you won't laugh?'

'Not if you don't want me to.'

'OK.'

So I told him the whole story. He didn't laugh. He was quite sympathetic actually. Then somehow one thing led to another and I found I was telling him about Mum and Dad. And Cedric and Clare and the mess I'd made of everything. He was a good listener. I don't know what happened to the time. An hour went by like minutes.

We walked over to my bus stop together. He took my mobile number and said he'd ask the neighbours and if he found a single possible Henry he'd be in touch right away. Then he swung his jacket over his delectably fit shoulder and said, 'See you around.'

I watched as he made his way back towards the mall. *Perfection*. Oh, why had I made such a fool of myself?

chapter fifteen

Most of Sunday was spent in a miserable haze of self-recrimination. I kept on having these hideous flashbacks of the moment I'd passed Henry the card. He must've thought I was *such an idiot*. In fact, I spent practically the whole day catching up on homework as a penance, which just proves how bad I felt.

The next day I headed into school with my backpack crammed with completed assignments. I even caught an earlier bus so I didn't have the usual mad dash to avoid being on the late list.

I arrived at the same time as a herd of swots. Hump-backed like wildebeests under their heavily laden backpacks, they made for their usual browsing grounds in the library. Not wanting to be categorised as one of them, I lingered outside. I was loitering in the school car park when I saw Mr Williams's car nosing into a space. He climbed out, and then who should climb out behind him but Ms Mills! I couldn't wait to tell Clare.

I waited by her locker till she arrived.

'You're in early,' she said.

'Yes, and you'll never guess what I saw!'

'What?'

'I was just passing the car park when Mr Williams's car drew up.'

'And?'

'And guess who got out?'

'Mr Williams?'

'Mr Williams *and* Ms Mills.'

'No way!'

'No, really, honestly.'

'Body language?'

'Hard to tell. She had on her green quilted parka – you know the one that sticks out all round and makes her look like a caterpillar.'

'What about him?'

'Too far away, couldn't spot any love bites.'

'Gross!'

The bell went for double English at that point, providing an opportunity to study Mr Williams at closer range. I even took a front desk so I could get an uninterrupted view. He walked in and took his place at the teacher's desk. He looked very pleased with himself: well scrubbed, positively pink and well-shaven. Catching sight of me, he said, 'Excellent performance of *Mother Courage*. Thank you for the ticket, Jessica. I do hope you'll get a chance to see it yourself.' Then he smiled at the class in an unusually benevolent way and asked us to get out our set books.

We were studying *Tess of the D'Urbervilles* and Clare was asked to read a passage aloud. I'd finished the book over the weekend and I was only listening with half an ear as I mused about Tess and Angel. Why had the whole relationship gone so disastrously wrong? He and Tess were a perfect match. Angel was all high ideals and love of nature and Tess full of youthful innocence and country purity.

A + (hi + lon) = T + (yi + cp)   *Good Match!*

It all hinged on a lost letter . . . Nightmare! The very thought brought back a horrible sick feeling as I relived that excruciating experience with Henry . . . *Henry*!!!!! I could feel myself going hot and cold all over.

Mr Williams's eye was upon me. He'd noticed my lapse in concentration. 'So Jessica? Would you like to comment on the passage Clare has just read?'

'Errm . . . ' (O-m-G. What passage?)

'Yes, Jessica?'

I had to say something. 'I think the book would have been so much better if Angel had found the letter in the first place,' I said all in a rush.

I could see Mr Williams was making a big effort to be patient. 'An interesting point of view. So what would have happened, do you think, assuming he had?'

'Well. I reckon that if he'd found the letter before they got married, he would have forgiven her.'

'Wouldn't that have ruined the plot?'

'No, it would've made it much better. You could have a brilliant bit about them both going off to become missionaries together in Africa. And none of that gloomy bit when she has to harvest swedes in the rain and it all gets so despressing . . . ' I glanced at his face. 'Errm.'

Mr Williams was sitting back in his chair gazing at me with an unreadable look on his face. 'Tell you what, Jessica. How about you writing a chapter of your alternative version for us. Let's say you start with Angel finding the letter. And then we'll compare them.'

'But Mr Williams—'

'It seems a pity to waste such an imaginative approach,' he said firmly.

'Yes, Mr Williams.'

'Right. Now, anyone else? Charlotte, how do you feel about Angel's reaction to Tess's confession?'

I fumed. I had enough homework as it was. He was being a huge pain.

I had a real moan to Clare in the canteen at lunchtime. 'A whole chapter! How does he think I'll find the time?'

'So what do you reckon now about your brilliant scheme to get him and Ms Mills together?' she asked.

'Well, he went to the play. He said so.'

'Hmm.' Clare took the tiniest mouthful of yogurt and licked the back of her spoon delicately. 'But how about her? We still can't be sure they actually met up.'

'True.'

Later that day, however, when I was passing the art room on the way to an English period I had confirmation. Ms Mills's handbag was open on her desk. I texted Clare straightaway:

rendevous confirmed
spotted mc programme in
ms m's handbag!
love j

I was in the cloakroom, standing at the mirror congratulating myself, when someone came up behind me.

'Hi.' It was *Christine*. Christine never spoke to lesser
mortals like me. She took out a brush and started to
waft it through her perfectly straight and shiny hair.
'Don't you live at Rosemount Mansions?' she asked.

'Yes. Why?'

'There's that boy who lives in your building . . . '

'In Rosemount? What boy?'

'Cedric something.'

'*Cedric?*' (What did Christine want with Cedric? I
couldn't be hearing this.)

'It's just that he has this session at this club Matt
goes to.'

'Cedric. Do we mean the same Cedric? Darkish
hair, skinny, square black glasses, kind of dweeby.'

'But *cool* dweeby,' she said, turning to me.

I stared at her. Cedric was *cool* dweeby? 'Cedric has
a session at a club?'

'Yes, I thought you knew him.'

'I do – sort of.'

'He's into some really good stuff. I wondered if he could make me a compilation tape?'

'Of *jungle*?'

'It's a surprise for Matt's birthday.'

'Ah. Huh.' (Cedric was cool. Jungle was cool. He was a DJ in a club. This was seriously worrying. Was I getting out of touch?) I gave her his number.

'Thanks, I'll see you around.' She swept out after that.

I stared at myself in the mirror. Suddenly it was me who was the dweeby one. Cedric had somehow metamorphosed into something so ultra-cool I hadn't even recognised it.

The equation had slipped the other way. If Cedric was cool dweeby, Clare was going to have to redouble her efforts. Currently, Cedric was cool dweeby, a DJ and into jungle. While Clare was still in her double brace and tracksuit bottoms and devoted to Victoria Beckham. Or, to put it scientifically:

$$Ce + (cd + DJ + j) > Cl + (db + tb + dVB)$$

Or to simplify:

Cedric > Clare

How was I ever going to turn that into Cedric ♥ Clare?

I caught up with Clare in the games changing room. She was currently doing double rounds of circuit training twice a week.

'Did you know Cedric was a DJ?'

'Oh, he did mention it. He does this session at a club on Wednesdays.' (I don't think Clare recognised the seriousness of the situation.)

'But don't you see what this means? He must think he's the coolest thing on two legs.'

'I know.'

'Has he been in touch?'

'Not exactly.'

'Have *you* rung *him*?'

'No, but . . .'

'But *what*?'

'I did text him.'

'What did you say?'

'Oh, nothing really.'

'Come on.'

'Just that I was hoping to hear from him.'

'Oh Clare, honestly. What did we agree?'

'But he hasn't and time's running out.'

'Look, from now on, you don't call him, you don't

text him. You don't even answer his messages.'

'Not answer his messages? Won't he think that kind of odd?'

'No. You've got to bring out a male's competitive instinct. The higher you value yourself, the more he'll want you.'

'Oh, I see . . . ' said Clare doubtfully.

I went home that night with more homework than ever. Just when I thought I'd caught up, Mr Williams had given me a whole chapter to write. *A whole chapter*. That would take for ever. I let myself into the flat, ready to have a good moan and get a nice hot meal and a sympathy session from Mum.

The flat was dark, empty and silent. Mum wasn't there. There was a note stuck to the fridge with a magnet.

Crisis on play
Emergency rehearsal
Fish fingers and peas in freezer
Back whenever
X Mum

Fish fingers and peas and no sympathy. And it was all Mr Williams's fault. What an ego-tripper. Anyone would think he was running the Royal Shakespeare Company the way he carried on. I grumpily defrosted the fish fingers and put them in the frying pan. Bag came and wound himself round my legs, mewing.

'We've been abandoned, Bag. Nobody cares.' How anyone could be expected to write a chapter of a book on a meal of fish fingers. A whole chapter! I bet Thomas Hardy hadn't. I bet he'd had one of those vast Victorian feasts – like pheasant and grouse and port jelly and suckling pig before he wrote his.

This was so unfair. Mr Williams didn't take it out on other people like he did on me. I was going to show him this time. I opened my file and selected a pristine sheet of paper and started writing:

In the gloaming, Angel climbed the rustic stairs to his lonely room for the very last time. All around, in the dark fields, the cows were breathing their sweet breath into the night air. All was quiet, save for the doves cooing gently under the eaves . . .

The silence was broken as he stumbled on the mat uttering a muted curse . . . (No, not Angel, not a curse . . . Errm . . .) *'Bother,' he exclaimed, rearranging the mat.*

Oh, but what could this be? A letter addressed in Tess's simple childish hand. He tore it open.

Dearest Angel,

There is something I must confess to you afore I can be yours . . .

At this point there was a ring on our doorbell. I went to the door and opened it.

'Hi!' It was Cedric. The last person I wanted to see. I still hadn't figured out what to say about that text message.

'Hi.'

'What are you up to?'

'Homework. It's a really important assignment actually.'

'Oh right. I won't stop then. I just had to talk to someone . . . It's about Clare.'

Clare! He wanted to confide in someone. (Sweet! At last, I was getting somewhere.)

'The assignment can wait. Come in,' I said.

'You're her best friend. Has she said anything to you?'

'Errm . . .'

'I'm really worried about her,' he continued. 'I don't know what the matter is. She's acting so weird.'

I nodded sympathetically.

'She won't answer my text messages. She ignores my calls. I don't know what I did but for some reason she doesn't seem to want to speak to me.'

'Oh dear.'

'And she keeps getting these really creepy texts from some *pervert*.'

'Pervert?'

'Yeah. What kind of creep is going to send a message like this?' He looked really embarrassed when he told me what it was. (Maybe I'd gone a bit far with that one.)

'It's no wonder she's going anorexic.'

'Anorexic?'

'Yes. Haven't you noticed?'

'Well, I knew she was on a diet, but . . .'

'She's gone all kind of pale and limp and weak-looking.' (This wasn't at all what I had in mind.)

'You think?'

'Yes, I think she needs help.'

'I'll talk to her.'

'You'd better. It could get serious.'

'Don't worry. I know Clare. I can deal with it.'

'Well, if you're sure.' He turned to leave. 'Oh, and by the way. I just wondered . . . if you're not doing anything on Saturday 2nd June.'

'Saturday 2nd. No idea, why?'

'It's this dance thing at school.' (O-M-G. No! Not the Cranshaw Memorial Ball!) 'I wondered if you were free that night . . . '

I couldn't be hearing this. Things had gone terribly wrong. He'd obviously taken my text message for *real* encouragement. 'Me?' I said stupidly.

'Well, yeah. It's no big deal. My mum bought the tickets. She kind of insisted. It's black tie and a bit cheesy, but . . . '

(Me! A horrible vision of Clare's face hearing me saying I had been invited instead of her rose before my eyes.)

'Errm. The 2nd. I'm not sure.' (I was thinking hard. If I said I wouldn't go with him now, he had time to invite someone else. No. The best policy was to stall him until it was too late.) 'I'll have to look in my Filofax. Can I let you know?'

'Sure thing. No worries. So you'll suss out Clare. Find out what's wrong?'

'Leave it with me.'

I let him out, feeling despondent. I returned to my essay but I didn't start writing. I just sat there desperately trying to think of a way to twist Cedric's invitation round to substitute Clare for me.

I lay in bed that night totting up my successes and failures. Whichever way I totted, the failures seemed to win. Nothing seemed to be going right. With Dad away I wasn't making any headway on the Dad = Mum front. Clare and Cedric were a disaster. And I wasn't getting *anywhere* with Jane and Henry.

But maybe there was a glimmer of hope. There was still Henry in Forest Vale. He might ring me, or text me. I felt hot and cold all over at the thought of it. He was so-oo gorgeous.

chapter sixteen

I really couldn't face Clare. I took the early bus again to avoid spending the journey with her. I managed to keep out of her way till lunchtime.

She was in the canteen ahead of me. On seeing me she waved violently, indicating that she'd kept a seat free for me at her table. Feeling like a traitor, I slid into the seat opposite her. She was pushing salad around with her fork. She'd only taken lettuce and tomato, no potato and not even a shred of grated cheese. O-m-G. What if Cedric was right?

'You'll fade away if you don't eat something soon,' I started.

'I don't care, as long as I get into that dress.'

'But you've got to eat.'

'Why?'

'Because you'll get all pale and limp and weak-looking if you don't.'

'No I won't.'

'You will. And then *no one* will want to go out with you.'

Clare stared at me, her eyes brimming. 'That's what you really think?'

'Yes. I mean no. I mean, honestly Clare, you were fine how you were.'

'And now I'm pale and limp and weak-looking and no one wants to go out with me. Is that it?'

'No!'

She was getting me really worried now. I'd heard about girls becoming anorexic. It started like this, with a diet that somehow becomes an obsession – and then they won't eat anything. Frightening! And I was responsible because I was the one who had set her off. What should I do now? Apparently, the last thing you do is try to make them eat. So I tried another tack. I did a big reassurance job, ending with, 'And I'm *sure* Cedric is going to invite you to the ball.' (I was damn well going to see to it that he did.)

Clare's dimples reappeared. 'So you'll come with me after school?'

'Sure. Where to?'

'To Top Knotch. To get the dress, of course.'

I swallowed a huge mouthful of food. I could feel

it going down in a lump in my throat. 'Don't you think it's a bit risky buying it before he's actually asked you?'

The dimples disappeared. 'So you don't think he's going to invite me?'

'Yes. Yes, I do.'

'I better get it then. The time's up – they won't hold it any longer.'

I went with her in a last-ditch attempt to put her off.

The dress was still there. The assistant had kept it aside as promised.

'Isn't it beautiful?' said Clare.

'You'd better try it on,' I said, stalling her.

'I'm just about to.' She picked up the hanger and headed for the changing rooms. I followed. Clare was already climbing out of her school uniform.

'How are you going to afford it?'

'I've saved all my birthday money. If I get a loan from Mum I can pay her back in instalments.'

'What will you do for spending money?'

'Look, Jessica. Can't you see? This is really impor-tant.' She was squeezing herself into the dress. There was no way the zip would do up.

'Can you kind of hold it at the back? she asked. She stared at the mirror and stood on tiptoe. 'There's still two weeks to go. It'll fit by then. What do you think?' she asked.

I hadn't the heart to be critical. 'What are you going to do for shoes?' I said.

'I don't know. Buy some. Dye some. Borrow some. I'll think of something.'

Even my advice to put a deposit on the dress instead of buying it outright went unheeded. I raised an eyebrow as she paid for it with a cheque.

'It'll only mean a nasty letter from the bank,' she whispered. 'I'll put the money into my account as soon as I can.'

I went home with my mind in a turmoil. This was getting worse and worse. And there was Marie's party coming up. Cedric and Clare were going to meet up there. What would happen if Cedric let on that he'd invited me to the ball instead of her? She'd be suicidal. She'd probably never eat anything ever again. She'd get thinner and weaker and paler and nobody would be able to do anything about it. What if she starved herself to death? It would all be my fault. Oh, why had I raised her hopes like that? But I'd been so sure that they were right for each other.

I'd have to think of some way round the problem before the party.

That Saturday Dad was back from his holiday. So we were able to have our weekly afternoon together as usual.

It was a really sunny day. Hot for the time of year. He was early for once. I caught sight of him waiting by the lake. As he turned I almost did a double-take. Was it Dad? He'd had his hair cut. The way I'd been going on at him about for years. Really short. Up until now, he'd had this weird notion men get when they think they're going bald, of growing it longer wherever it grew, to compensate – mainly at the back and sides. Which makes the balding bit on top stand out like an egg on a nest. But short like this, it made the bald bit kind of blend in. He was tanned too, from the holiday, which helped.

'Like the haircut,' I said.

'Yes, well. Thought I'd give it a try. How's my favourite girl?' He gave me a hug.

'Hey, you're less cuddly too.'

'Been off the beer,' he said. 'On the vino though.'

I noticed he was wearing a new blue shirt that

brought out the blue in his eyes. He looked suddenly years younger. 'Your holiday's done you good. Got any pics?'

'Umm . . . ' he said. 'Not developed yet. Show you next week.'

'So, what shall we do this afternoon?'

'Want lunch?'

'Too nice a day to sit inside.'

'I've got the bike over there. Why don't we go for a spin somewhere.'

'Wicked.'

He took a fiver out of his pocket. 'You go down to the kiosk. Choose us some sarnies and drinks and we'll make a picnic of it.'

I came back from the kiosk to find him talking into his mobile. He clicked off when he saw me.

'Who was that you were you talking to?' I asked.

He ignored my question. 'How would you like lunch at the Gran' Paradiso next Saturday?' he asked. (The Gran' Paradiso does the most yummy spaghetti carbonara.)

'Mmm, great. What's the celebration?'

He winked at me and clicked open his mobile again. I heard him booking a table for three – by the window. For *three*. My heart did a double somersault.

It was all falling into place. I knew it. He was going to ask Mum.

'So . . . ?' I asked.

He grinned in a sheepish way. '*So* . . . what?'

'Aren't you going to tell me what this is all about?'

'Wait and see!' he said. He handed me his spare helmet and I climbed on the bike behind him.

We had the most fantastic afternoon. It was a glorious spring day – clear blue skies and sunshine. We rode out to somewhere called Banstead Beeches which looked like the kind of pictures you get in a calendar – all fresh young green leaves and dappled shade.

Dad parked the bike by a lake and we ate our sandwiches. The sun was really hot and when we'd finished we stretched out for a while basking in the warmth of it. Afterwards we found some flat stones on the lakeside and had a competition playing ducks and drakes. Which Dad won, as always.

Then we walked for a couple of hours. The paths were deep in leaf mould that gave off a sweet musky scent. Dad was in a really good mood, telling daft jokes. It was just like old times. At the end of the day, we found a tearoom – really oldy-worldy, all oak beams and lattice windows. It was warm enough to sit with the window open letting in the late afternoon sun. Dad ordered a slap-up tea with hot crumpets.

'I'm really looking forward to next Saturday,' I said, encouraging him to talk.

He winked at me. 'Good,' he said.

Then he glanced at his watch. 'Better be making a move.'

'It's not going to be dark for ages. Do we have to go so soon?'

'I've got to be back by seven. Meeting someone.'

'Who?'

'Never you mind.'

He dropped me off at Rosemount. Mum should have been back from her rehearsal but the flat was empty. I thought I'd make us dinner as a surprise. I raked through the fridge and found some onions and a red pepper. Just what was needed to make us her favourite spaghetti sauce with chilli in it.

It was eight by the time I'd finished making the sauce, and Mum still wasn't back. 'Meeting someone,' was what Dad had said. Could it be Mum?

I decided to have a bath and wash my hair while I waited for her. I lay in the hot water fantasising about what it would be like if they got back together. They might even have another child. A brother or sister for me. Mum had kind of hinted at it.

At nine I heard her key in the lock. I wrapped myself in my towelling robe and made my way into the kitchen. Mum was humming tunelessly to herself. But tune or no tune, I hadn't heard her hum in ages. She looked happy. 'Had a nice afternoon?' she asked.

'Brilliant. We went to Banstead Beeches.'

'Glad you still get on with your dad,' she said, giving me a hug.

'Why shouldn't I?'

'No reason at all. He is your father.'

'I made us dinner. Your favourite.'

'Dinner?'

'Yes, I'm ravenous, aren't you?'

'Oh, I hadn't thought.'

'Have you eaten?'

'Umm, sort of. I had a sandwich in the pub.' (There you are. Mum eating in a pub. She hated pubs. It was Dad who always ate in pubs. Dad had been meeting someone at seven. And Mum was late back . . .)

'Pub? I thought you were at a rehearsal,' I prompted.

'I was. The pub was afterwards. What've you made?'

'Spaghetti arrabiatta but I haven't cooked the spag yet. Which pub?'

Mum started distractedly filling a saucepan with water and adding salt. 'Oh, the one near the hall where we rehearse. Why?'

'No reason. How did it go?'

'What?'

'The rehearsal.'

'Oh, that, yes. Not bad. Not bad at all. Pass me the salt,' she said.

'You've already put it in,' I pointed out.

'Oh, so I have,' she said, dipping a spoon in the water and tasting it.

I looked at her curiously. She was more absent-minded than ever tonight. Must have something on her mind. She strained the spaghetti but said she didn't want any. 'Save me some of that lovely sauce for tomorrow,' she said and wandered off.

I poured parmesan on my spaghetti and dug in. Why didn't she confide in me? I wondered. She'd hardly had a chance, I realised. I hadn't spent any time with her in ages.

'Mum?' I called. 'Do you want me to test you on your lines?'

'I think I'll have a bath and go straight to bed,' she said. 'I'm really tired. Incidentally,' she added, 'you are going to come and see the play, aren't you?'

'Of course.'

'We're having a party afterwards. I really want you to be there.'

'A party. It'll be all your amateur dramatic friends. I won't know any of them.'

'Well, this is your opportunity. Anyway, you know George.'

'Mr Williams. Pl-ease!'

'Honestly, Jessica . . . '

'OK, which night is the party?'

'The final night. The 2nd.'

(The 2nd! Excellent! The excuse I'd been waiting for. Now there was no way I could make the Cranshaw Ball.)

'OK, I'll be there,' I said.

I went to my room plotting how to tell Cedric. I'd better not tell him right away or he might invite some other random girl. I needed to find precisely the right moment so that I could be sure that Clare was in the front of his mind.

Through my bedroom wall I could hear Mum in her room talking on her mobile. Which was really extravagant, not like her at all. She always used the house phone. There could be only one reason for that – she didn't want me to hear who she was talking to.

When she came out of her room she had a secretive expression on her face. I bet it was Dad.

On the way to school that Monday I felt I had to tell someone. I confided in Clare. 'Guess what. I think Mum and Dad are going to get back together.'

'No,' she said, her eyes round. 'What makes you think that?'

'Oh, lots of things. Hints, phone calls, I think they met up last night in a pub.'

'What's made them change?'

'Well, I might have had a bit to do with it,' I said modestly.

'Really, how?'

I didn't give her a full rundown, just the gist of how I'd subtly engineered the whole thing: like getting Dad to join a gym and talking Mum into her make-over and . . .

'You make it sound so easy,' interrupted Clare, then she stared out of the window. I bit my lip. Maybe it was tactless of me to go on about Dad and

Mum like that. But Clare seemed to have lost interest. 'Oh my God, look at that,' she said, craning out of the window. She was staring down at the bus stop below us. Ms Mills was standing there in her raincoat.

'It's Ms Mills, so what?'

'But *look*.'

A car I recognised as Mr Williams's had drawn up alongside and she was climbing into it. 'So he's giving her a lift to school.'

'Which means,' said Clare. 'When we saw her getting out of his car the other day, it didn't mean they'd spent the night together. It didn't prove a thing.'

'No. I suppose it didn't.'

'I thought that was another of your matchmaking triumphs,' she said in an unusually off tone.

'It doesn't prove anything either way,' I said. 'I still reckon they're made for each other.'

Clare was really off with me all day at school. I reckoned it must be because she was starving herself. I always get cross when I'm hungry.

At lunchtime, I realised how dependent I'd got on her. I couldn't see her anywhere in the canteen. I actually had to sit at a table with a couple of the swots.

I could see them sort of eyeing me uncomfortably and wondering what I was doing there. Then one of them leaned over and asked, 'Is your friend all right?'

'Who, Clare? Yes, I think so. Why?'

'You usually sit together, that's all.'

'Yes. I suppose she isn't hungry.'

'So she's OK then?'

'She's fine,' I said, trying to sound more confident than I felt. (O-m-G. Everyone was noticing now. And she hadn't even come down to lunch. It must be serious.)

I didn't see her all afternoon. And at the end of the day she didn't wait for me in the cloakroom so I had to go home on the bus alone.

Mum got back from her rehearsal that night with a worried look on her face. She took a load of flyers for the play out of her bag.

'What's up?'

'Tickets aren't selling. We'll have to cancel if we haven't got an audience.' (Huh. Serve Mr Williams right, I thought.)

'Could you give some of these out? We've got to drum up an audience somehow.'

'I suppose so. I could take some into school.'

Maybe I'd find someone who'd be interested. At least I reckoned Ms Mills would want to go. In order to make absolutely sure, I took one of the handbills and added in scrolly writing:

Saturday 2nd, Celebration Party After the Play with Free Wine and Refreshments.

Next day I found Ms Mills by the photocopier.

'Did you know Mr Williams was a famous play-wright, Ms Mills?'

'So I've heard,' she said. 'He's very modest about it.'

I handed her one of the flyers. 'He's got a play on next week, my mother's in it. He wrote the whole thing,' I said.

She looked at the handbill. '*Six into Eight Won't Go*, by George Williams. How very clever of him,' she said. 'I certainly won't miss that.'

I went down to the canteen feeling a glow of achievement. I was relieved to see that Clare was there for once. I decided to be all calm and cheerful and act as if nothing was wrong. I got my tray of food and breezed into the seat opposite her.

'Guess what? Ms Mills is going to Mr Williams's play,' I said.

'So?'

By her tone I could tell that she was still being a pain. 'Well, that must prove something.'

'She's keen on plays?'

I ignored her sarky tone and said, '*And* keen on Mr Williams.' I made a big act of enjoying my meal of lasagne, hoping she might relent and go back for some. 'Mmm, this is really yummy. Is that all you're having?'

She eyed my plate with a pained expresson. All she had in front of her was a natural 100% fat-free yogurt and an apple. 'Yes.'

I ignored her hostile look and said on a more positive note, 'It's Marie's party on Friday.'

'I know.'

'Cedric's going to be there. What are you going to wear?'

'Not sure yet, why?'

'Anything but beige,' I said.

Clare looked really hurt. 'What's wrong with beige?'

'Beige is the kind of colour you just can't get worked up about.'

'What do you suggest?'

'Black. Black's always flattering.'

'You *do* think I'm fat, don't you?'

'No!'

I got home that night to find Mum muttering to herself in the kitchen.

'Everything OK?'

'It's this one long speech. Keeps coming out like gobbledegook.'

'Want me to test you on it?'

'There's something more important, if you've got time. You wouldn't be an angel and go round the building and see if you could get rid of some of these tickets, would you? There are still loads left . . . '

'Sure. I'll do it after supper.' (It had occurred to me that this would be the ideal way to get Roz and Jekyll together. I could get Mum to invite them to the party afterwards. There's nothing like a party to set things in motion . . .)

I started to wash salad, only listening to Mum with half an ear as she moaned on about the play. 'There's only a week to go till the first night. And the last act is still a disaster. George says we've got to rehearse all next Saturday . . . '

I dropped the salad spinner with a clash. 'Saturday? But you can't . . . '

'Why ever not?'

'Because . . . ' I started. 'I thought you were having lunch with Dad.'

'With *Dad*. Whatever gave you that idea?'

'I don't know,' I muttered. (I had a horrible sinking sensation in my stomach. If Mum wasn't having lunch with us, who was?)

I left Mum to prepare the meal and went to my room. I called Dad on my mobile.

'Dad, tell me the truth. Who are we having lunch with on Saturday?'

'Someone I'd like you to meet.'

'Someone?'

His tone changed. 'Look, Poppet. I'm human, you know. I need friends.'

'Friends'? Maybe it was some bloke, I thought wildly. Some mate of his from the pub.

'Well. A friend. A special friend.'

'A girlfriend?' I asked. I swallowed. (I'd known it would come to this some day. But I'd always put off thinking about it.)

'I think you'll like her.' Dad was laying it on. 'I'm sure you will. She's a great girl. A fun person. Not like your mother at all.'

'What do you mean?'

'No, for God's sake, I didn't mean that. Of course, your mother's lovely and fun too in her own way. But Mandy isn't serious like, you know, like . . . '

'*Mandy?*'

'Short for Madeleine.'

'Dad, you can't possibly go out with someone called *Mandy*. How old is she?'

'Old enough. Why the cross-examination? You'll meet her yourself on Saturday. Come on, Poppet. Give your old dad a chance . . . '

'You're not old,' I said.

'Precisely. So cheer up, eh? Nice meal at the Paradiso. Saturday should be fun.'

'Mmmm.' I clicked off my phone and sat down on my bed. So, Dad had a girlfriend. A *girl*friend. A *fun person*. Mandy. Yukk! *Mandy!* But it didn't have to be for ever, did it? It was just some girl. Someone to go out with for a while. Have *fun* with. It could even do him good. Couldn't it?

I decided to put the problem to the back of my mind until I'd actually met *Mandy*. You never know, if she was so awful, it might make Dad realise what he was missing not being with Mum.

chapter seventeen

That evening I did a tour of the whole building with the tickets. Practically everyone said they'd like to come. Madame Zamoyski was delighted. She hadn't been to the theatre for years; but she didn't know how she would get there. This was easily solved by Colonel Mustard, who lived opposite. He said he'd be only too delighted to give her a lift in his car.

Jekyll actually asked me in. Hyde was in the kitchen doing the ironing. Jekyll, who was actually called Barry, said he and Hyde (Jeremy) just adored the theatre and as it happened they were both free on that night.

Roz said she'd come if she could find someone to baby-sit. The Serial Killer was out and so were several other people. So I just left the tickets in their mailboxes with a note. All in all, I got rid of twelve tickets, which I reckoned was quite an achievement.

* * *

The following few days, however, were fraught with tension. I had to avoid Cedric because I knew if we met he'd be bound to ask about the ball. Which was tricky seeing as we lived in the same building. I got to be able to estimate which floors the lift stopped at simply by timing the noise it made. And I checked religiously who was calling before I answered my mobile.

Somehow we got to Friday – the night of Marie's party – without an encounter. I just hoped and prayed that when the right moment came I'd be able to get Cedric alone. Then I'd kind of slip the idea of inviting Clare instead of me into his head – as if he'd thought of it himself.

I'd arranged to go round to Clare's so that we could get ready together at her place. I was going to make sure that Clare looked brilliant if it was the last thing I did.

Clare was in better spirits when I arrived. 'Tonight's the night!' she announced, pumping tea-tree bodymist all over herself. She started taking umpteen things out of her wardrobe and holding them up against herself. 'What shall I wear? It's really important,' she said.

(She was so right.) We went through her entire

wardrobe before we settled on the optimum combi-
nation. I had her dressed in a pair of flattering black
jeans and my favourite black top, and I went over her
hair with her mum's heated hair tongs. Just as we
were ready to leave, her mum came in to say she'd
made us some supper.

'There'll be tons to eat at the party,' Clare
objected.

'Bowls of crisps, I expect. You get something inside
you.' Her mum insisted, so we both sat down at the
table. I ate the spaghetti bolognese she'd made. It was
scrummy. But Clare emptied hers into the bin when
her mum wasn't looking.

'You'll be starving later,' I remarked.

'No I won't.'

The party was in full swing when we arrived. We
could hear the music from way down the stairwell
and the neighbours had already started complaining,
which is always a good sign. Clare and I forced our
way past a load of hopeful gate-crashers and made
towards the source of the music. The room was full
of gyrating bodies. To my relief, Cedric was nowhere
to be seen.

Marie must have asked practically everyone from

our year. They were all crammed into the first room. The girls, minus school uniform but plus make-up and heels, looked twice as old as the boys. While the boys, curiously transformed, mostly by hair gel, were sadly the same dweeby boys as ever.

A group of Cranshaw boys was in the second room and only the most confident girls – like Christine – had ventured in. She was already entwined with Matt. I peered through the doorway but Cedric wasn't there either.

'So where is he?' demanded Clare.

'Maybe he's not here yet,' I said. 'You get in there and start dancing. When he turns up, I'll bring him in. Whatever you do, make sure you don't look interested. Make out like you're having a fantastic time and he doesn't exist.'

'Right,' said Clare and she started dancing enthusiastically right beside Antony – dweeb-of-the-year. I sighed. Would she ever learn?

I came across Cedric in the kitchen. He had somehow landed himself the job of opening bottles and pouring drinks and was currently pegged behind the kitchen table which was a-swill with a multicoloured cocktail of spilt liquid. Brilliant, I'd got him on his own.

'Hi!' I said, squeezing my way through a jam of

thirsty people to get to him.

'Jessica!' he called out, looking ominously pleased to see me. 'Want to dance?'

'Errm, not really.'

'Nor do I. Let's find somewhere quiet.' He clambered out under the table, sending a tidal wave of slops over the waiting crowd. 'Uh, sorry,' he said.

We squeezed our way out into the corridor and found ourselves kind of wedged between the kitchen and the bathroom. People kept weaving their way back and forth. I practically had to shout. The music was deafening.

'Cedric, listen. I've got to talk to you,' I said.

'What?'

'Look, I'm sorry. I can't go with you – to the Cranshaw Ball . . . '

'You can't?'

'No, I've promised Mum. I've got to go to see her play.'

'Her play? Can't you go another night?'

'It's the final night. Mum wants me to go to the party afterwards.'

'Oh. I see.'

'But you could take someone else.'

'Mmm.'

I moved a little closer. This was it . . .

'Listen Cedric. Why don't you take Clare? She really wants to go. And I know she's free that night . . . And she's got this dress and everything and . . . ' I tailed off. Cedric was looking over my shoulder. He gave me a warning glance.

'Thanks a lot . . . ' It was Clare's voice behind me. I swung round. She was right up close to me. She must have heard every word.

'I don't need you to arrange my social life for me, Jessica, thank you very much,' she said. 'And just for the record,' she added, turning to Cedric, 'I wouldn't go with you if you were the last male on earth.' Then she stormed into the bathroom.

'Now look what you've done,' said Cedric.

I went after her. She slammed the door in my face and locked it. I banged on it. 'Clare, open up. Let me in. Please.'

'Go away,' came her muffled voice through the door.

'Listen, Wobble . . . '

She flung open the door and glared at me. 'Don't ever call me Wobble again.' And she swept past me. I watched as she snatched up her coat and left the party.

'That's done it,' said Cedric.

'Oh my God. What shall I do?'

Terrible visions of her throwing herself under a car, or out of a window, or off the top of a building, swam before my eyes.

'I'll go after her,' said Cedric.

I watched over the bannisters as he ran down the stairs two at a time. 'Clare . . . Clare . . . listen . . . '

The door slammed behind them.

I didn't stay long at the party. I felt too guilty and miserable. I got a mini-cab home and called Clare up on the way. She didn't answer my call. *Where was she?* I left a humble text.

so sorry
i should mind my own business

That night I had a weird dream in which Clare had turned into a slither of herself. I mean she looked like Clare from the front, but sideways she was thin enough to slip between the floorboards. I woke with a shock. What if Clare starved herself to death and it was *all my fault*?

Mum came into my room at some excruciatingly early hour the next morning. It was barely light. 'I'm just off to the rehearsal. How did you go with the tickets?'

The events of the night before flashed through my brain. I pulled the duvet up over my head with a groan. Mum was insistent. 'Come on, wake up. George will need to know how many are left.'

So I rose on one elbow. 'Tickets?'

'Yes.'

'Errm. I got rid of about twelve I think. The rest are on the kitchen table.'

'Well done. So where's the money?'

'Money?'

'Money, cheques, whatever, for the tickets.'

I was wide awake now. 'People didn't have to *pay* for them, did they? I thought they were comps . . . '

'Jessica, honestly. How do you think we can afford to put on a play if we don't sell tickets?'

'I don't know. I mean, I thought it would be better to have an audience than no one . . . '

'Well, you'll just have to think again. You'll have to go back and ask those people for the money. Someone's going to have to pay up.'

'Oh dear.' I pictured Madame Zamoyski, she'd been so delighted. And Roz who didn't have a bean to her name. And Jekyll and Hyde, I mean Barry and

Jeremy – they didn't look too well off. I lay back in bed miserably wondering how much I had in my post office savings account. I heard Mum go out and close the door rather more firmly than usual behind her. Bag climbed on to my bed and rubbed himself against me, purring furiously. I drew him to me and buried my face in his fur.

Everything was going wrong. To top it all, *nightmare*, today was the day I was due to have lunch with Dad and *Mandy* at the Gran' Paradiso.

chapter eighteen

I arrived at the Gran' Paradiso before them and was shown to a table in the window, so I saw them arrive. Dad parked the bike half up on the curb and then '*Mandy*' climbed off.

I don't know if my jaw actually dropped. But it did metaphorically. I suppose you have to wear a short skirt if you're on the back of a bike. That's unless you're wearing trousers of course. Which might've been a better idea in the circumstances.

I tried my best not to stare as Dad stowed his and Mandy's crash helmets. Mandy had the kind of legs that looked as if they'd spent their entire life on stilettoes – like the ones she was currently wearing. Muscular. I guess they needed to be to support the rest of her – she was a big girl. Her mini-skirt was topped by a cropped jeans jacket that was flashily mock stone-washed in bright white creases.

Underneath I suddenly caught a glimpse of . . . No! I didn't believe it. *She had a ring in her belly-button.* Now that was just so unfair. The double standards of parents. Dad went absolutely ape when I wanted to have my ears pierced. And that was only *ears*.

But Dad steered Mandy in ahead of him with an expression on his face like the cat that had got the cream. The Italian waiters did a predictably Italian double-take at the sight of her. But Mandy's attention was elsewhere. The Gran' Paradiso was one of those restaurants which economised on windows and made up for it by covering the walls with mirrors. Mandy was currently taking full advantage of them. She tossed her hair at the first and then glided by the others giving herself loving half-glances with a fixed mirror-face pout.

'Hello Poppet,' said Dad, giving me a hug. 'I want you to meet—'

'Jessica!' interrupted Mandy. 'My . . . don't you look just like your dad?'

'Hello,' I managed to smile. (I didn't look a bit like Dad. It was Mum I looked like.)

There was a painful pause. Dad was shuffling from foot to foot and rubbing his hands. Was I meant to get up and kiss her? But no, thank God, he was drawing out her chair and making false-sounding 'Isn't this place lovely?' noises, which was really embarrassing seeing as he'd chosen it. I mean, the Gran' Paradiso is fine because of the food and everything, but they do have really dire false flower arrangements and the kind of flouncy blinds that Mum calls French knickers.

'Well, how are things?' asked Dad when we were all seated. He stared at me pointedly, willing me to speak. I tried not to catch his eye. Luckily, the waiter came along and provided a welcome diversion by handing out the menus.

'So, let's have some drinks then. Bottle of rouge? Coke for you, Jessica?'

'I'll have a Campari-soda,' announced Mandy. I couldn't help noticing that this was the most expensive drink on the drinks list. Dad ordered a beer to keep her company.

'Oooh,' said Mandy, studying her menu. 'Look Ted, insalata tutto mare! We haven't had that since—'

Dad interrupted. 'Great. Why don't we start with that?'

I said that I'd be happy with a spaghetti carbonara. 'Oh, but you must have a starter. Try the insalata tutto mare,' said Mandy.

'No, really I—'

'Come on, Poppet. Give it a try,' said Dad. There was an edge in his voice. I could see I'd have to give in. So I shrugged in agreement.

An awkward silence descended which was broken by Mandy. 'That's a nice colour on you, Jessica. That top you're wearing,' she said. 'I've gone mad for pale blue this spring.' (God, was she was struggling to find common ground.)

'Thank you.'

'She suits it, doesn't she Ted?'

'Yes!' said Dad. As if pale blue was the most amazing colour anyone had ever worn.

'We ought to go shopping together some time,' continued Mandy. 'I love shopping, don't you?'

'Umm, it depends . . . ' I said, staring at my plate. Visions of myself done-up to look like Mandy flashed through my mind.

Dad stirred uncomfortably on his chair. 'You know you enjoy shopping, Jessica. All girls do.'

'Maybe I'm not like *all* girls . . . ' I said rather too quickly.

Dad glared at me. At that point, with welcome timing, our food arrived. I picked at my salad, wondering what the white bits on the top could possibly be. Some vegetable perhaps, cut in rings. I cut off a tentative piece and chewed. It tasted like old car tyres. Mandy was busy calling the waiter over to ask for fizzy water.

'What is it?' I spluttered to Dad.

'Octopus,' he whispered back.

What I had in my mouth was *horrible wobbly tentacles*. The room seemed to go all slurry before my eyes and I felt really sick. 'Excuse me,' I muttered, pushing my chair out. I ran for the loo and spat it out.

I stayed in the cubicle wondering if I was going to be sick or not. Wild thoughts were racing through my mind. How long had Dad known her? My mind kept going back to the belly-button ring. And I suddenly knew what was odd. She and Dad were exactly the same colour. As if they'd got a tan at the same time. This couldn't simply be a coincidence. Mandy must have gone to Spain with him, which meant . . . My mind did a terrible calculation. Did Mandy plus belly-button ring and flashy mock faded denim equal Dad plus his Harley-Davidson and his black leathers:

$$M + (bbr + fmfd) = D + (HD + bl)$$
Match or Mismatch? I thought wildly.

There was a knocking on the cubicle door. 'You all right, love?' Mandy had come to find me.

'Fine, thank you,' I said. I flushed the loo and came out of the cubicle.

'Ooh, you do look pale. Do you want me to stay with you?'

I shook my head. Mandy was wearing this really strong perfume. She seemed to be filling the space between the basin and the hand-dryer. All I wanted was for her to leave me alone.

'No, I'm really OK. You go back. I'll be with you in a minute.'

When I got back to the table, Mandy wouldn't leave the subject alone. 'You must be allergic,' she said. 'Allergic to seafood. Lots of people are. Aren't they Ted?' Then she started to list the things she was allergic to. She went on and on talking about food which made me feel worse.

I managed to catch Dad's eye and whispered, 'Would it be all right if I left now?'

'If you really don't feel well.'

'She can't go home on her own, Ted. Look at her.'

'Yes I can. A walk in the fresh air will do me good.'

But Mandy insisted on calling a taxi. The taxi took ages to come. I didn't feel like eating anything, so I had to sit there sipping fizzy water while Mandy rabbited on about star signs and how she could tell I was an Aries right from the start. I reckon Dad must've told her when my birthday was.

I felt really sick in the taxi. I kept on getting the taste of octopus in my mouth.

As soon as I got home I rushed upstairs and cleaned my teeth and washed my face in cold water. I wished Mum had been there so I could tell her all about it – about the meal and the octopus and how terrible Mandy was. She'd understand.

I spent the afternoon laid out on the sofa watching an old black and white movie on TV. I wanted Mum to come back and reassure me that it was just a passing phase and that Dad would be back to normal soon. They both would. Back to how they used to be, like in that photo Dad had hanging up to dry. It seemed such a long time ago now. But there was still hope. They weren't divorced yet.

After an hour or so, Dad rang. 'You OK, Poppet?'

'It was only the octopus.'

'So . . . ?' he said.

'So what?'

'So maybe the lunch wasn't such a good idea.'

'No. I don't think it was.'

'Listen, Mandy's a great girl when you know her. Why don't you spend some time alone together? Girl stuff. I want to buy you a nice outfit as a present. For that party of your mother's after the play. You know what I'm like, I can't choose. Why don't you go shopping with her, like she suggested?'

'Do I *have* to?'

'Of course you don't *have* to.'

'But you want me to.'

'I'd like you to be friends.'

'I'll think about it.'

At last, I heard Mum's key in the lock. She let herself in and dumped her bag on the floor. 'Nice lunch?' she asked brightly.

'Not very,' I said.

'I'm exhausted. Be a love and make us some tea.' I heard her take off her coat and hang it up and then she came into the kitchen and watched as I filled the kettle. 'What's up?'

'Did you know about Mandy?' I asked. I didn't *mean* it to sound like an accusation.

'Oh, *Mandy*, yes. Yes, yes I did. So Ted's introduced you.'

'Why didn't you tell me about her?'

'I thought your dad should.'

'Dad *can't* like her. She's hideous.'

'Is she? I wouldn't know. What's so hideous about her?'

'*Everything.*'

'Come and sit down,' said Mum. I followed her into the sitting room and sank into a chair. My legs were feeling wobbly and I had a big hard lump in my throat.

'You've known about her all along, haven't you?' I forced out.

'Come on. Tell me. What's so dreadful about her?'

'She's . . . she's not like us. You'd hate her. She wears these awful clothes like they're years too young for her. Stuff I'd wear. No, stuff I *wouldn't* wear, 'cos it's really horrible. And . . . and she's got a belly-button ring and Dad wouldn't even let me get my *ears* pierced . . . ' I tailed off.

'Well, maybe he'll have to now.'

'I don't want to have them pierced any more.'

'Jessica, aren't you forgetting something?'

'What?'

'Maybe she's what your dad needs.'

'How do you mean?'

Mum then went into a long monologue about how we had to let Dad make a new life for himself. I was only listening with half an ear. I wanted her to scream and rant and sound Dad off. How could she be so calm about it?

Apparently, Dad had met Mandy down at the gym. The very one I'd suggested that day at the bus stop. Mum said she thought Mandy had been really good for him. In fact, apparently, all those things I'd been congratulating myself on, like him cutting down on booze and giving up smoking and taking more exercise, had been down to Mandy all along. She was his *fitness instructor*.

'Haven't you noticed how he's making an effort? He's looking so much better and—'

'Huh,' I interrupted. 'Fitness instructor. She didn't look particularly fit to me.'

Mum gave me a look. 'Didn't she?'

'No.' I was near to tears now. I got up and turned my back on Mum. Clearly she was taking his side. Nobody seemed to care how I felt. I went to my room with my mind in a turmoil. I had to speak to someone. I desperately needed Clare. But she still wouldn't answer my calls so I sent another text.

need to talk to you
desperately
j

Almost immediately she texted me back:

no way
c

I stared miserably at my mobile. She must be really mad at me. This wasn't like Clare. When we argued she'd flare up but she'd usually calm down. Generally, within an hour or so, we could laugh the whole thing off.

I went into school on Monday determined to make it up with her. But she wasn't on the bus. Her coat wasn't hanging in the cloakroom. And she wasn't in English either. Apparently her mother had rung in. She was off sick.

Off *sick*. My heart did a lurch. Then it hit me with the full force of conviction. Cedric was right. She'd been pale and limp and weak-looking and now she was *off school*. It was anorexia. I had this sudden horrible vision of her lying in bed, white as the sheets, too frail to move. And then later laid out on the Murphys' dining-room table with a candle at each end and me coming in with a huge bunch of pink gladioli (her favourite flowers). No, not gladdies, it would have to be something more mournful, like lillies perhaps. Yes, huge white scented lillies. I'd visit her tomb every spring and put gladdies – no, lillies – on it.

'Jessica?' Mr Williams's voice broke through my sombre thoughts.

'Yes, Mr Williams?'

'How did you get on with your *Tess of the d'Urbervilles* chapter?'

'Umm. Fine thank you, Mr Williams.'

'Well, would you let me have a look at it?'

'Yes, all right.' I located it in my backpack and handed it over to him. Mr Williams cast a critical eye over the page, frowned and put it in his briefcase. I knew it wasn't a very long chapter but Mr Williams didn't realise what I was up against. It was all very well for Thomas Hardy. He hadn't had the problems of reuniting his parents, curing an anorexic best friend and solving a love triangle when he wrote his version.

* * *

As soon as I was out of class I hid in the cloakroom and dialled Clare's mum. She answered right away.

'Yes, Jessica?'

'I just wondered, Mrs Murphy, how's Clare?'

'Well, I really don't know. I've called the doctor, as a matter of fact.'

'The doctor?' I repeated weakly.

'I don't know what's got into her. She hasn't been eating properly for weeks. I found all her dinner in the bin the other night.'

'Can I speak to her?'

'She's asleep at the moment. But she said she didn't want to speak to anyone.'

'Oh, I see.' I clicked my mobile off. She'd called the doctor, so it must be serious. I felt like a criminal. Oh, why had I let her go on a diet?

For three agonising days Clare didn't come into school. She wouldn't answer my calls and I ran out of cheery things to say in text messages. I rang Cedric but he had become strangely elusive too. I even went down to his flat a couple of times but each time his mum said he was out. She didn't know where. Maybe he was sitting by Clare's bedside holding a limp hand. Oh Clare, how could I have done this to you?

The rumour about her being anorexic had gone

through the school like wildfire. People kept coming up to me and asking about her as if I was the eye-witness at some sort of national disaster. The swots had sympathetically taken me into their group and insisted I sat with them every lunchtime, which was really kind of them but incredibly humiliating all the same.

chapter nineteen

After three agonising days, worried sick ... on the fourth, Clare was back in school.

I didn't actually see her till lunchtime. I caught sight of her across the canteen. Actually, she didn't look too bad from a distance, considering she was at death's door. I got my tray of lunch and approached cautiously. She was eating. I'd have to be really really careful not to put her off.

I coughed gently. 'Hello ... Clare.'

'Mmm.' She looked up.

'Would you mind? I mean, would it be all right if I sat here?'

She nodded with her mouth full. I slid in opposite her. She continued eating without saying a word. In front of her was a huge plate of beef stew and mashed potato. She was shovelling it in as if there was no tomorrow. *Beef stew and mashed potato!* And after the way I'd been worrying about her?

I took a tentative mouthful of my salad, wondering who would be the first to break the silence. Then she looked straight at me and came out with one of her perfect dimpled grins. She pushed her plate away. There was hardly a trace of gravy left on it.

'God, I needed that,' she said.

'You could've called me. I was really worried about you,' I complained.

'It was only a virus,' she said.

'A virus. I thought you were practically dead.'

'I laid it on a bit. I wanted to be sure I'd be fit for Saturday.'

'Saturday?'

'The Cranshaw Ball.'

'He's asked you?'

'Yes. As a matter of fact.'

'I knew he would.'

Clare looked at me archly. 'How?'

'Well, you're really made for each other.'

'You'd got it all worked out, hadn't you?'

'Yes. I mean no.'

'You can't run everyone's life you know, Jessica.'

'I know. I mean, I don't want to.'

'Good, because basically, both Cedric and I feel you've interfered.'

'Me? Interfered?'

'In fact, we were so mad at you I reckon it kind of bonded us . . . ' said Clare. The dimples reappeared. Then she told me in detail how brilliant Cedric had been and how understanding he was and how he'd caught up with her and walked her home after the party and stayed with her and talked for hours because she'd been in such a state.

'So you see, you've me to thank after all, haven't you?' I said.

'In a round-about way, yes, I s'pose I have.'

'And you can wear that dress after all.'

'That dress was rubbish. I took it back. It was way too small anyway. And I found this brilliant funky dress with this cerise lining that kind of shows when it's . . . '

Christine wafted by at that point. She leaned towards Clare. 'Will you tell Cedric thank you from me. Matt just loved the compilation. See you at the ball.'

'I'll let him know,' said Clare.

Clare and Christine, talking to each other! And they were all going to the ball and I wasn't. And Clare was getting a brilliant funky dress. Hang on a minute – I was starting to feel really out of it.

* * *

That afternoon I came across Mr Williams in the corridor. He was adding a banner to his *Eight into Six Won't Go* poster on the Arts Activities noticeboard. TICKETS STILL AVAILABLE. *Sad.*

'How's my most talented pupil?' he asked, catching sight of me.

'Most talented, Mr Williams?'

'I really liked that piece on *Tess*. You should use that imagination of yours, Jessica.'

'Thanks, Mr Williams.'

'I think we could count it as coursework, don't you?' He reached into his briefcase and handed me back my chapter with a smile. He'd given me an A+ for it. The writing down the side was surprisingly positive, at least I think it was. He said that I'd written a nice 'pastiche' of Hardy.

I slipped into the library and looked up the word 'pastiche' in the *Oxford English Dictionary*. It said: '*Literary or other work of art composed in the style of a well-known author.*' Uh huh. Literary! Perhaps Mr W was able to recognise true talent after all.

It was just as well I had literary talent because socially I was a total disaster. That Saturday while everyone was getting ready for the Cranshaw Ball, I was due to go shopping with my dad's hideous girlfriend to get an awful dweeby outfit for my mum's excruciatingly uncool amateur dramatics party. Dad had it all worked out. It was blackmail really. He said that if I went shopping with Mandy, he would spend the whole day with me on Sunday. Just the two of us. I could stay over at his place on Saturday night and he'd do breakfast, lunch, everything. So I'd agreed.

I made my way into Mandy's leisure centre with foreboding. Mandy was already seated at a table in their coffee shop waiting for me. I wondered if I ought to offer to buy her a coffee. But she didn't give me a chance – she leaped up and got me a cappuccino with a double dose of chocolate powder on top. She was obviously bending over backwards to get me to like her.

'Isn't this fun. Where are we going to shop then?' she asked.

I suggested the usual places I bought my clothes at but she pooh-poohed them. 'No, your dad said to get you something really nice. Let's go to Top Knotch.'

'But everything costs a fortune there.'

'Come on, Ted won't mind. It's for a special occasion,' said Mandy. Some 'special occasion' I thought, taking a sip of my coffee. It was sickly sweet – I don't like sugar in my coffee.

'Don't you like cappuccino?' asked Mandy.

'No . . . yes. It's fine,' I said, choking it down.

'Come on then. We're wasting precious shopping time,' she said and got to her feet.

'How much did he say I could spend?' I asked.

'Leave it to me,' said Mandy. She gave me a wink.

As soon as we entered Top Knotch, I knew it was a mistake. The racks were hung with really extreme designer clothes. Everything was covered in lacings or ruching or embroidery or whatever. It was the kind of stuff that shouted out 'fashion victim' the moment you entered the room.

Mandy was in her element. She kept holding things up against herself and pouting into the mirror. 'This is cute,' she said, handing me a blue jeans jacket that had sequins and cerise feathers sewn all around the collar.

I shook my head. I'd found a rack with some bootcut black jeans that weren't too bad.

'Black,' said Mandy with a frown of disapproval. 'It's so last year.'

Luckily the next load of racks held clothes that

were much too old for me. But Mandy steamed on ahead, sifting through a selection of evening wear that was far too dressy. I lagged behind in the teenage stuff checking the price tags. I could feel myself coming out in a prickly heat rash. I couldn't let Dad spend money on me like that.

Mandy rejoined me and despite my protests started to gather an armful of stuff for me to try on. Everything she selected I hated. An assistant had noticed that I was coming under pressure. There weren't many people in the department and before I knew it another had joined her. Like lionesses that single out the weakest in the herd, they were closing in. The two of them started to do a really hard sell on a pair of snakeskin-print hipsters. Mandy agreed with them. I tried to say that I never wear stuff like that. It was getting really embarrassing.

'Well, we've only got half an hour before I've got to get back to work,' announced Mandy. 'I really don't believe that you can't find *anything* in a huge department like this.'

In the end, Mandy practically frog-marched me into a cubicle and said she'd be waiting outside to pass judgement. The first thing I tried on was a sick turquoise colour that made me look completely washed out. Then I squeezed into some shiny white Lycra separates that made me look like some poor sad wannabe. I stood there with my socks hanging in folds round my ankles staring at my reflection. I was starting to feel like a freak.

'Now this is more like it.' Mandy must have taken the opportunity to go on another foray. Around the curtain came a T-shirt top that was luminous green with kind of multicoloured Smarties all over it. 'Look, it's got a mini-skirt to match.'

Under her strict instructions I tried it on. 'Let's have a look,' she pestered when I was half-in, half-out. I emerged from the cubicle. She and the assistant went into ecstasies. It was so *now*, it was so *new*. It made me look *taller-slimmer-older-cooler*. I slipped back into the cubicle and checked the price tag. It was on sale – the cheapest thing I'd tried on. I sighed. I'd promised Mum I'd dress up for the party.

'All right,' I said weakly. 'I'll take it.'

I went home fuming, with the outfit in a Top Knotch bag.

'What did you get? Let's have a look,' said Mum.

'Don't ask. Mandy talked me into it.'

'Well, I hope it's something you can wear tonight.'

'It'll have to do. We ran out of time.' I dragged the outfit out of the bag. It hadn't looked such a hideous colour under the shop lights.

'A bit kind of wacky, isn't it?' said Mum holding it up.

'It was in the sale. Everything else cost a fortune.'

'I suppose it's quite fun for someone your age.' (I shuddered at that word, 'fun'.)

'According to Mandy I look brilliant in it. And she seems to think she's the world's greatest fashion expert. A belly-button ring at her age. Sad case. And she hasn't even got a particularly flat tummy.'

'Hasn't she?'

'No.'

Mum paused and looked at me oddly. Her next statement came like a bombshell. 'That's probably because she's pregnant,' she said.

'*Pregnant.*'

'I thought you ought to know before you made a total enemy of her.'

My head reeled. 'Mandy's having a baby?'

Mum nodded. I stared at her as the full realisation sunk in. '*Dad*'s baby?'

'Which means that you'll have a brother or a sister,' said Mum in a falsely cheery voice. 'You know you've always wanted one.'

'How does Dad feel about it?' I asked weakly.

'He says he's really pleased.'

'I see.'

'Do you mind very much?'

'I don't know. I'll have to think about it. A *baby*. What's going to happen. About you and Dad I mean?'

Mum continued speaking, but I could tell by her voice it was really difficult to talk about. 'They want to get married. So we'll have to sort out a divorce. That's what we've been talking about. We didn't want to tell you until we'd both made up our minds.'

'And now you *have* made up your minds?' I asked sitting down at the kitchen table. I hadn't noticed but I'd been screwing up the Top Knotch receipt in my hands. It was all in bits. Now I'd never be able to change the outfit.

'Come on, it's not as bad as all that,' Mum said, putting an arm round me. 'It was bound to come to this in the end.'

'Don't *you* mind?' I said.

'I've got used to the idea now.'

I didn't know how Mum could be so accepting about it. I felt as if the bottom had fallen out of my world. Everything I'd been hoping for and dreaming about had suddenly disappeared into thin air.

* * *

I tried ringing Clare but she'd left her mobile on message only – probably too busy getting ready for the ball. I had to speak to someone. So I went downstairs to see Cedric. I rang on his doorbell.

'Can I come in?

'Sure . . . Hey, what's up?'

'Everything.'

'Come on,' he said, leading me into his room. He turned off the music. 'Come on, tell me. What's going on?'

'It's all gone wrong. My dad's got this girlfriend . . . '

'Uh huh.'

Cedric didn't say much. He just let me ramble on. He was a really good listener. 'And now she's pregnant . . . ' I ended. 'And Dad wants a divorce. So Mum and Dad'll never get back together again.'

'But your parents were really miserable together, you said so.'

'I know, but I thought that if they changed, you know all the things that made them mad at each other, well, things would be different.'

'Why do you want them to get back together?'

'Because they're my mother and father, of course.' It was out of my mouth before I'd even thought about it.

259

'Jessica. Is that a good enough reason?' I fell silent. 'Hey, come on, think it through. Look at the positive side. I'd love to have a brother or sister.'

'Would you?'

'Yeah. We could take it out. When it's big enough. Take it to the zoo and stuff.' That was really sweet. I was starting to understand what Clare saw in him. I suddenly realised I'd been gabbling on about me and hadn't even asked about her.

'Clare told me you're taking her to the ball tonight,' I said. 'And she's eating again. Like normal.'

'Yep. I think we've sorted a few things out.'

'She was really angry with me.'

'We both were.'

'I was only trying to make things better—'

'Said the dictator.'

I had to laugh at that. I went back upstairs feeling happier. I still had this kind of empty sore feeling inside – and yet there was something else as well. An odd kind of feeling that I couldn't quite identify. I'd always longed for a brother or sister. But I didn't expect it to happen like this.

chapter twenty

Thanks to me, practically the whole of Rosemount Mansions was going to Mum's play that night. There were three car-loads of them. Mum had to leave early to get ready for the performance, so I was getting picked up by Dad *and Mandy*. Dad had it all worked out. He reckoned it would be best if Mum and Mandy met on neutral territory – and the play would be the ideal thing. Plenty of distraction to keep them occupied. I reckon I was being taken with them as a kind of hostage to keep the peace.

Being driven there, in the back of Mandy's car, I felt really sorry for myself. Clare and Cedric and everyone were dressing up and going to the Cranshaw Ball while I was being forced into watching Mr Williams's cringe-worthy amateur play with Dad and my nightmare future step-mum.

The play was in Forest Vale Community Centre

(Mecca of sophistication). And, as if all that wasn't bad enough, I had to be dressed up in my lurid Smarties outfit to please Dad (*and Mandy*).

Forest Vale Community Centre was absolutely jam-packed when we got there. It seemed the last night was a sell-out. There was even a queue of stragglers at the door asking if there had been any returns.

I spotted Ms Mills ahead of us. 'Great turn-out, Ms Mills,' I said. 'Mr Williams should be pleased.'

She beamed at me. 'I think I may have had something to do with it. I photocopied the handbill you gave me and circulated it.' (I had a fleeting vision of the bill I'd scrawled on: '*Free wine and Refreshments.*' Oops!)

There was a lot of scraping of chairs as people assembled and then the lights went down and the pianist started a kind of overture. Silence fell on the hall. The curtain was drawn back with a set of fits and jerks and the stage lights went up, revealing a courtier in doublet and hose. I settled down resignedly in my seat as he started on his opening speech.

'*Now in the merry month of May,*
Methinks the king should marry
We'll scour the globe for ladies fair
To please our noble Harry.'

(Yawn! I knew it would be terrible.) I cast my eye
around the hall. In the gloom I could make out
Colonel Mustard and Madame Zamoyski who were
listening intently. Roz had arrived late and was now
sitting on the end of our row beside Jekyll and Hyde.
I even spotted the Serial Killer in the back row.
There were several teachers from my school – Ms
Mills's influence I imagined. And there were a load of
guys in the front row looking a little restive.

My mind wandered as another courtier joined the
original one and there was a lot of talk of treaties and
battles and other tedious historical stuff. *Double*
yawn! I wondered how Clare and Cedric were getting
on at the ball. Christine would be there with Matt
too. I bet they were all having a wicked time.

My attention was drawn back to the action by a
kind of bugle fanfare. And then striding on to the
stage, padded out to a tremendous girth, complete
with ruff and beard, came *Mr Williams*. He was holding a portrait miniature in his hand.

'*Foresooth, the widow of my brother!*
England's queen shall be no other
Methinks we'll marry Catherine of Aragon
Fair of face – of virtue a paragon . . . '

But no sooner had he married Catherine, than there was a lot of fuss about the church and annulling the marriage – all pretty tricky to handle in verse. You'd think Mr Williams could have found something better to rhyme with 'divorce' than 'horse'. Eventually Catherine was supplanted by Anne Boleyn. I sat there aching with boredom wondering when Mum was going to come on.

There was a brief interval when everyone got up and stretched their legs to the accompaniment of a lot of scraping and clunking from backstage. Then we sat down again for the second act. The scene had been set with a painted backcloth of trees and shrubs, and a pot of rather obviously false flowers had been placed centre stage to indicate that this was meant to be a garden.

Mum entered carrying a basket with cut flowers in it. I hardly recognised her under her wig. Her costume looked really good in stage lighting. The way the false gems glittered made them look almost real.

'*Fairest Jane, I want to make you mine*
Pray answer me
Let me hear your voice divine . . . ' said Mr Williams.

'*Henry . . . My King* . . . ' replied Mum.

Somewhere deep in my brain some loose connection joined up and . . . O-m-G!!!!! I didn't hear the rest of the speech. *Jane! Henry!* This couldn't be just a coincidence, could it? The card was *in verse* too and the handwriting . . . *That's* why it was so *curiously familiar*. I normally only saw it in *red*. O-m-G. There could be no doubt about it, *Henry* was Mr Williams and *Jane* was *Mum*. The purple envelope hadn't got misdirected. It was meant for Mum all along.

My mind then did an extremely complicated calculation. Did Mr Williams minus padding and ruff and beard plus terrible rhyming verse plus measly teacher's salary plus clapped-out-car equal Mum minus wig and wimple plus OU English course minus hopeless cooking and housekeeping plus delinquent daughter and fat cat?

MrW – (p + r + b) + (trv + mts + coc) = M – (w + w) + OUEc – (hc & h) + (dd + fc)
Ple-ase God NO?

No, no way! Mum was lovely and Mr Williams was a pain. Mum was always on my side and Mr Williams was always down on me. It was just as well that I had intercepted the card before it got to her.

At that moment I felt my mobile vibrate in my pocket. I brought it out. In the dim light I could just make out that I had a text message.

found j & h!
see you later
henry

It was from the Forest Vale Henry!!!!!! I texted him back straightaway.

where are you?
j

I sat with my head in a whirl through the rest of the play. At last the actors were taking their bows. The lights in the hall went up and people started to disperse. At least, some people left. There seemed to be a lot who were staying on for the party.

But I had something more important on my mind. Henry from Forest Vale had texted me. Where was he? How could I find him? And who were the Jane and Henry he had found?

My train of thought was interrupted by people trying to shift me so they could move the chairs. Tables were being set up with bottles and glasses and plates of nibbles. The actors had started to appear from backstage and were mingling. Mum came out front dressed in her normal clothes again. She actually went up to Dad. I watched them out of the corner of my eye. He put an arm around her and kissed her on the cheek and turned her towards *Mandy*. She was talking to her now. She was *laughing*. They both were. I couldn't help staring. How could they be so calm about the whole thing?

'Hi,' said a voice right beside me which made me nearly jump out of my skin. It was Forest Vale Henry, standing there large as life.

'What on earth are you doing *here*?' I gasped.

'Last minute panic. Guy who does the lighting had an accident. I stood in. What are you doing here?'

'My mum. My mum's in the play,' I said.

'Oh? Who's she playing?'

'Jane Seymour,' I said, feeling incredibly stupid.

'Oh,' he said, and then he thought for a moment. 'Ah, I see. That explains it then. About the card, I

267

mean. Why it turned up at your place.' He looked at me sideways. 'You don't look very pleased about it.'

'Mr Williams is my English teacher.'

'So?'

'He's a real pain.'

'George? No he's not. He's a laugh. At least, he's OK when he's backstage.'

'Is he?' I said, wishing that I hadn't made such a fool of myself. Wishing that I wasn't there with my mum and my dad and my future step-mum like some kid. Wishing that I'd worn anything apart from my hideous Smarties outfit.

'Can I get you something to a drink?' he asked.

I nodded. 'A Coke if they've got one.' He joined the queue at the refreshments table.

My mind was racing. What about Mr Williams? The *real* Henry? The Henry who'd sent the card. He was after my mum. Mr Williams who I saw nearly every day of the week, in his saggy sports jacket and down-at-heel Hush Puppies. *Mr Williams* wanted to *marry* my mother? It couldn't be true. Could it?

It was difficult to keep him in my sightlines. There was a constant stream of people coming between us. Everyone wanted to go up and congratulate him. But in the brief glimpses I had, he didn't seem to be suffering from unrequited love. On the contrary, he was standing with a glass of wine in his hand being extremely jovial. And Mum was now carrying plates round, helping to serve the food. She was smiling. She certainly didn't seem to be fading away from love sickness. In fact, she seemed unusually happy.

Mum = Mr Williams   *No way!*

Delectable Henry came back with our drinks at that point, so I decided to put the whole thing to the back of my mind until later. It was quite a good party actually. There were far too many people and no way near enough to drink or eat. But someone put some music on and turned the lights down and I spent quite some time dancing. Mainly with Henry as a matter of fact. And he said he'd like to see me again. *And that maybe we could meet up for a film or something next Saturday.*

To which I could only think:

H = J   *Perfect Match!*

Or to simplify even further:

J ♥ H

So really everything had turned out absolutely *PERFECT*.

Except . . .

There was one thing haunting me. I still had the problem of *the purple envelope*. I couldn't get it out of my mind until I'd destroyed it.

chapter twenty-one

Dad didn't want to spend long at the party because Mandy was feeling tired. She dropped us off at Dad's place. I got out and waited tactfully by the lift while they said goodnight.

Dad had made a real effort to make me feel welcome. He'd cleared out his photographic gear from the spare room and even put a couple of pictures on the wall for me. He said he'd make us both frothy cocoa like he used to when I was little. I sat in the kitchen and watched while he made the milk bubble up in the saucepan. I could tell he was waiting for me to say something about Mandy, about the baby, about the divorce, but the words kind of stuck in my throat.

'You're very quiet,' he commented.

'I'm tired too.'

'Yes, course you are, Poppet. Been a long day.

Plenty of time tomorrow, eh?' He handed me a mug of cocoa.

'Thanks. Do you mind if I take it to my room?'

'Course not.' He gave me a big hug. 'Sleep tight.'

'You too.'

But I didn't sleep tight. I tossed and turned in the narrow put-you-up. I couldn't seem to get comfortable. Visions of the purple envelope kept zooming round my mind. Every time I was about to drop off to sleep it would swing round again – and again and again – taunting me.

I got up eventually and crept into the kitchen to make a cup of tea. Dawn was already breaking. The sky was all peachy-golden. It was going to be a fine day. What if Mum woke early? What if she went into my room while I wasn't there? I could imagine her now, looking in my drawer for something – socks or whatever, she was always borrowing mine. And finding the envelope. She might be there right now. I could picture her, taking out the card, groping for her glasses . . . *I had to get home to stop her*.

Without bothering about the tea, I slipped into my room and dressed. The trains started running at about seven on a Sunday, I could easily be back home before Mum was up. I found a biro and a slip of paper and left Dad a hurried note to the effect that I'd be back for brunch.

The station was deserted on a Sunday morning. I was the only person waiting for the train. It seemed to take ages to come. My stomach was churning. All I could think of was destroying the card.

At last the train arrived. Within fifteen minutes I had got out at our station. I made my way through the deserted streets and ran up the steps into Rosemount. As quietly as I could, I let myself in through our front door feeling like a criminal. I slipped into my room. Bag stirred on the bed and looked at me sleepily but mercifully didn't miaow. Sliding open my drawer I took out the purple envelope and drew out the card. '*To someone special.*' That was so naff. I opened it and shuddered as I read the verses.

In life as in art
You've stolen my heart . . .

Mr Williams and my mum – no way! With determination I tore the card into the tiniest pieces.

Now what? I stared at the pieces guiltily. This was like disposing of a body. I couldn't simply put them in the bin for fear of Mum finding them. And I couldn't burn them for fear of the smoke alarm going off. So I put the pieces in an envelope and stowed it in the bottom of my backpack to dispose of later.

Bag leaped down from the bed and started winding himself round my legs. I picked him up and carried him back. I lay down burying my nose in his soft fur. He purred delightedly and kneaded the covers with his paws. I lay there stroking him. And I started thinking about Mum. Now she and Dad were getting divorced, she'd be all on her own when I left home. I mean, I couldn't stay for ever. I'd leave Bag with her, I resolved. But cats didn't live that long. She might never meet another man who'd fall in love with her. And she'd get older and sadder. When she was too old to go out to work she'd be marooned here in the flat. I imagined her shuffling around in terrible slippers. What if the lift broke down . . . ?

And then I thought maybe Mr Williams wasn't *that* bad. I remembered how he'd been nice about my *Tess of the D'Urbervilles* chapter. '*My most talented pupil*' he'd called me. Then another echo of his voice went through my mind: 'Just for the record, Jessica, there is no "c" in plonker.' But actually, that was quite cool of him, when you came to think about it.

And then I started feeling really, really guilty. Maybe I shouldn't have torn up the card. It wasn't addressed to me, it was to Mum. Oh, why had I ever opened the envelope? If I'd just thrown it in my bin and forgotten about it no one would've been the wiser.

Eventually, I got off the bed and stomped over to my backpack. I took out the envelope with the pieces in it and found a roll of sellotape in my drawer. I'd really made a good job of tearing it up. It took ages to stick it back together again. When I'd finished, it looked like crazy-paving.

I could hear movements from Mum's room. I strained my ears. She must have gone into the kitchen to make tea. There was nothing else for it. It was confession time. With resolution, I took a deep breath and picked up the card. Mum didn't expect me to be at home and I didn't want to give her a fright, so before I went into the kitchen I coughed loudly. Then I opened the door.

But she wasn't the one who got the fright. I was. Because standing in the kitchen holding a tray with two mugs of tea on it – wearing Mum's towelling robe – was ... *Mr Williams.*

chapter twenty-two

Well, what more can I say? Nothing had gone quite the way I'd wanted it.

Or to sum up:

Mum + (amo + cs + nt) > Dad + (ow bb)
Mega Mismatch

Because:

Mandy + (bbr + fmfd) = Dad + (HD + bl)   *Match*

And:

$$\frac{\text{MsM} - \text{ph} + \text{gs} = \text{MrW} - \text{wc} + \text{nh}}{\textbf{a}}$$ *Mismatch*

Because:

**MrW − (p + r + b) + (trv + mts + coc) = Mum −
(w + w) + OUEc − (hc + h) + (dd + fc)** *Match*

And:

Cedric + (cd + DJ + j) = Clare + (db + tb + J)
Match

But!

**Henry + (sbe + fb + nsl + hcb + pfi + cli + lt) = Jessica
+ (nsbdh + ll + st + nfj + nbTs + dn)**
Match!!!!!!!!!

Or to simplify:

**Mum ♥ Mr Williams   Dad ♥ Mandy
Cedric ♥ Clare**

(Only most unfortunately I now realised: **Jekyll ♥
Hyde**. Which left Roz. But I *was* working on that . . .)

BUT most importantly of all:

Jessica ♥ Henry!

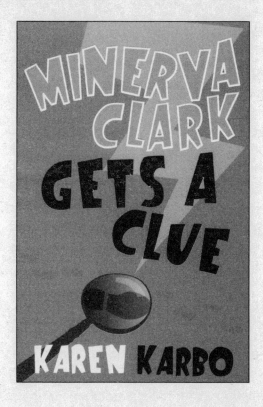